FIELD TRIP FAE

Uncle Chip Saves the Fae
Book 3

JAMIE DAVIS

MedicCast Productions

Field Trip Fae

By Jamie Davis

Copyright © 2023 by Jamie Davis. All rights reserved.

Cover design by CoversByChristian.com

This is a work of fiction. Any resemblance to actual persons living or dead, businesses, events, or locales is purely coincidental.

Reproduction in whole or in part of this publication without express written consent is strictly prohibited. The author greatly appreciates you taking the time to read his work. Please consider leaving a review wherever you bought the book, or telling your friends about it, to help him spread the word.

Thank you for supporting his work.

❀ Created with Vellum

Acknowledgments

This book made possible with the generous assistance of these Kickstarter Backers:

Kristi Preston-Barnes, Dom Graham, Jessica Spring, Martha Carr, Conrad J, Nic Anderson, Glen Errington, Christian "Mecki" Hejl, Gerald P. McDaniel, Ryan Scott James, Delia A Landstrom, Arveyah Wright, Merri, Brianna Welch-Martin, E.M. Middel, Mary Eleanor, Kathy D C, Deborah Snowden, Dr. Cindy Ann Simon, Rabbi Fred Natkin, Beth Jones, Carol Cha, Rec, Sue Byrne, Karen Johnson, Stephen Ballentine, Melinda Kucsera, Scott McConnell Distance CME, Sabrina Graham, Nan & Rick W., Jenn Mitchell, Renee Roberts

Rose

"Chip, duck!" I threw the dagger as hard as I could at the ravenous zombie running up behind him.

Chip hunched down and crouched just in time. The dagger embedded in the creature's eye. The zombie dropped, the now inert undead body skidding to a stop next to where Chip's crouched.

I whirled around and took up a two-handed stance with my sword. We'd stumbled into the necromancer's trap and there was no way out but through the remaining eight zombies coming at us.

"Chip, get up and come stand beside me. We can't let them get between us."

He stood and ran over to join me. He'd actually done pretty well in this fight. He'd held his own against the initial onslaught. I'd still had to save him from the one coming at him from behind, but that kind of situational awareness during a fight only came with lots of practice and more than a little actual combat.

Chip raised his Guardian sword and joined me in the room's opening. In theory, the narrow passageway limited the number of the crazed undead who could reach us. I hoped that remained true.

The charging zombies ran up to us and we began hacking at the clawing hands reaching out to drag us into their snapping teeth. The stench of their rotting flesh filled the air around us. It threatened to make me retch.

I fought back against my rebellious stomach and swallowed the rising bile in the back of my throat. I hacked off a hand reaching out to clutch at my face. We just had to keep ourselves away from their snapping jaws and teeth. I didn't relish the painful treatment necessary to ward off a zombie's bite.

"Remember, head shots are the only way to kill them."

"I remember, I remember," Chip called as he hacked at the zombie in front of him. His voice had risen in pitch a little, but he seemed to be holding himself together. The attack had surprised both of us.

Chip batted aside the hands trying to pull him closer and lunged in to thrust his enchanted blade through his zombie's mouth. The blade came out the back of the head, piercing the magically animated brain inside. The zombie dropped.

Unfortunately for Chip, it fell with his sword still wedged in the skull. He struggled to pull the blade free.

I cut through the neck of the one in front of me. The still-animated head toppled from the body even as the rest of the deanimated corpse collapsed.

Chip had a foot on the head of his previous target and yanked backward. The stuck sword came free suddenly. He lost his balance and fell over onto his ass.

I lunged to the side and pierced the ear of the zombie preparing to leap on Chip while he was down. I pulled back as soon as the creature went limp, making sure not to replicate Chip's mistake.

"Get up. I can't hold them alone." I took a step back in the passage, getting closer to the opening into the room behind us. I didn't want to give them a chance to get all around us like the first batch had.

Chip scrambled to his feet. He bent down to retrieve his dropped sword and then stepped back in to stand beside me.

"Sorry, Rose. I didn't know my sword would get stuck like that."

"Just." Hack. "Keep." Thrust. "Fighting." I ducked low and kicked out with my foot, sweeping the next zombie's feet out from under her. The undead woman toppled over and temporarily tripped up the ones behind her.

I leaped forward and stomped down with my black leather boot, crunching through the brain pan with my heel, killing the beast below me.

Chip moved up next to me, shoving back the zombie facing him with a kick to its chest.

The press of undead still threatened to overwhelm us and we were hard pressed to keep them from forcing us backward into the open room.

"Chip, try your force wall on them. See if you can hold them back while I try and figure a way out of here. There has to be a way out of that room back there."

"I can try." He held up his left hand while he kept the sword ready in his right. His face screwed up in concentration for a few seconds and then he grunted and leaned forward as if pushing on an invisible barrier. He had them.

I stepped back from where Chip stood keeping the zombies back with his Guardian magic. The room behind me was made of stone and cinderblock in construction. If there was a way to get out, it shouldn't be too hard to find. The necromancer had lured us into this basement room without windows or obvious doors. Unless he'd transported himself out by teleportation, there had to be another way to escape.

"Do whatever you plan on doing quickly, Rose. I can't hold them back for long. There are too many of them pushing back at me. I can feel the mana draining from my reserves."

"Just hold them, Chip. I'll find the exit. It has to be here somewhere."

I looked back at the entrance where he stood pushing at the zombies and then looked at the back wall of the empty room. We had chased the necromancer in here. When we charged in after him, he was gone. We could see the back wall, so which way did he go when he entered? I thought back and remembered the evil wizard turned left after running into the room.

The left-hand wall was all cinderblock which meant it was probably an interior wall and didn't lead outside. The stone foundation of the old Victorian home lined the outside basement walls.

I ran my fingertips along the wall, tracing the cement lines in between the cinderblocks. There had to be a seam somewhere in here.

There. A ridge passed under my tracing fingers, and I stopped.

I leaned forward and peered at the wall, trying to see with my naturally enhanced night vision abilities. The single old sixty-watt incandescent bulb in the middle of the ceiling did little to fill the room with much light. I leaned forward, staring at the seam. There was a narrow gap there. It followed the interlocking sections of the cinderblock.

"Rose, I don't know how much longer I can hold them."

I twisted to look over my shoulder. Chip had backed up a pace closer to the doorway. "Push at them, Chip. I've almost figured it out."

The wall definitely had an opening. I didn't see the mechanism that would unlock it, though. There had to be a release catch on this side somewhere. I searched all along the wall outside the area where the door was. There had to be a block to push on, or a hidden panel that opened up somewhere around it.

I kept looking, getting more and more frustrated by the second. The door had to have a method that opened it. It couldn't just push or pull open.

"I'm about done, Rose. Get up here. We'll have to fight them."

"I've almost got it, Chip. Just hold on."

"I don't have the power to give anymore. I'm almost dry."

My balled-up fist smacked on the hidden door, the anger at not being able to decipher the riddle overwhelming me. The section of cinderblock depressed about a half-inch then popped back towards me as my fist came away. The door now had a one-inch lip I could grasp. The whole door closed with a spring-loaded latch on the other side.

I gripped the edge with my fingertips and pulled. The door swung into the room with ease. It was just in time.

Chip gasped and dropped his trembling arm to his side. He stumbled back in my direction, barely able to lift his sword as he moved as fast as his exhausted legs would carry him.

"Into the opening. Hurry."

He half-stumbled past me. I backed into the opening and pulled at the handle on the inside of the faux cinderblock panel that was the door. I stabbed at the first zombie to reach me. I dropped it with a piercing blow to its head and yanked the door closed before any of the others could get there and block the opening.

Chip had collapsed inside the long hallway that extended away from the hidden door. I had pulled the door closed and it clicked as the spring mechanism engaged again. Hopefully, the zombies didn't press on it and pop it open while we ran away down this passage.

I helped Chip to his feet. He checked the closed door and saw there were no zombies close. He pressed the jeweled stud on his sword's hilt. The blade glowed blue and then collapsed and folded in on itself until he just held the leather-wrapped handle of the hilt in his hand. It was like something from a superhero movie. With the blade gone, Chip slid it into the custom leather sheath on his belt, now only six inches long.

Jealousy flared up in my chest like it always did when I saw his magical blade in action. I'd kill for a sword I could hide like that. I loved my longsword. It had been with me since it was awarded to me as a teenager. But I had definite blade envy at the magic that his sword had within it. The weapons smith had called it one of his masterworks and I couldn't disagree with him. It was amazing to see in action.

"We have to hurry," I said. I waved for Chip to follow me. "We might still be able to catch the necromancer. He had to go this way, too."

"He's got a head start on us."

"All the more reason to hurry. Can you keep up?" I looked back to see if he was there.

Chip moved at a fast walk and looked like he was about to fall over. "That mana drain took a lot out of me. You go ahead. I'll catch up."

"Okay, if there's a turn off that I take ahead, I'll mark it somehow. Otherwise, assume I kept going straight."

He waved at me to go ahead and slowed down to catch his breath.

I squeezed at the grip on my sword, trying to push some of the anger from my thoughts. It wasn't his fault he was so drained. It was his barrier that had allowed us to get away relatively unscathed. I shoved down my anger. We had to catch up to this sorcerer.

Warren, the werewolf investigator I used sometimes, had reported on the missing bodies from funeral homes, the county morgue, and some recently dug graves. It was a problem we didn't want in our quiet little corner of suburbia. We'd put together a profile and tracked down this new necromancer, though we didn't know exactly who they were. I wasn't going to let a threat like this develop in my back yard. It was the kind of thing that could distract me over time from my primary purpose, watching over Sadie. She was growing up so fast and I had to protect her with all I had.

The underground passage went straight for some distance. There were occasional lights wired and mounted in the ceiling that lit the way. Other than that, it was a plain concrete floor with cinderblock walls. No doors or side hallways branched off from the corridor and I ran along for at least two hundred yards before it ended in a cinderblock wall. I looked around for a way out and found one when I looked up. There was an opening in the passageway's roof. There, about ten feet above me through a narrow vertical shaft, was a trapdoor.

The problem was there was no way up there that I could see. I didn't think the necromancer had flown up there. All indications said he was human aside from the use of evil magic. There must have been a rope or a ladder, and he'd removed it to keep from being followed.

I tried jumping up a few times, using the wall below to kick up into the shaft. It wasn't any higher than a basketball hoop, so it wasn't that difficult. The problem when I reached up and touched the door at the top of my leaps was there were no handles on the trap door or anything else I could grip to pull myself up.

I was still trying to leap up and push open the trap door when Chip finally caught up to me. He slowed from a jog and came to a stop right as I landed with one knee bent to the floor in what I liked to call my action pose.

"What are you doing?" he asked as he leaned forward to look up the shaft.

"I'm trying to get up there. The guy must have pulled up the ladder."

He took a couple of deep breaths and then cupped his hands together. "Here, I can give you a boost."

"Okay, but just lift my foot." I sheathed my sword at my belt. "Keep your hands off my butt."

"Rose, I would never think of it." The twinkle in his eye showed his true feelings on the matter.

"Yeah, sure. Let's do this. He's getting away."

Chip bent down, interlaced his fingers, and I stepped into his cupped hands. He lifted me up while I steadied myself against the shaft's walls. I reached up with one hand and pushed against the trap door. It lifted a few inches on one side.

"Lift me higher. I can open it if you do."

He grunted more than I would have liked pushing me up higher. I wasn't that heavy. I was a Fae princess, after all. I almost said something about his lack of basic male strength but decided not to press the issue.

With my fingertips, I pushed the trap door open farther and gripped the wooden lip of the opening with one hand. I braced one foot on the wall while I pushed up with my free hand. It lifted me from Chip's outstretched hands, and the trap door flipped open to smack on the wooden floor above me. With my free hand on the opposite side of the opening, I pulled myself up until I could get a boot up into the room above.

I rolled to the side and climbed to my feet. The room looked like a work shed of some sort. There was an old, rusty push lawn mower in there along with lots of other yard and garden tools. Most were also as rusted as the mower and were covered in dust and dirt. This had been unused for a while and I'd think it was abandoned except for the shiny, aluminum ladder lying beside the hole in the floor.

"Hey, drop me a rope or something." Chip looked up from below at me when I leaned over the opening.

"Hold your horses." I levered the ladder up and lowered it down until he grabbed it from below. With that taken care of, I walked to the door and opened it. A farmhouse stood nearby across a yard filled with tall grass that hadn't been mowed in ages. I could see the outline of the neighboring Victorian home in the distance against the night sky. There were no lights on in the farmhouse and it looked abandoned. An old pickup truck sat parked by the house, but there was no sign of our quarry.

Chip oofed as he climbed out of the shaft and stood up inside the shed.

"You're out of shape, Chip. We're going to have to work on that in our training sessions. You've been missing a lot of them lately and it shows."

"It's hard. Sadie and Addy have soccer practice almost every weeknight and there's so much that has to get done during the day when they're at school."

"I don't care. You're the Guardian. You need to be up to the task of protecting Sadie from threats."

"Hey, I saved both our butts down there in that basement."

I shut up and looked around outside. The necromancer was long gone. "Come on. Let's go back to the car and head home."

Chip took a second to flip the trap door closed before he joined me outside.

I raised an eyebrow at his delay.

"Hey, we don't want some kid stumbling onto that opening and finding those zombies the hard way, right?"

He wasn't wrong and he knew it. He winked at me just to prove he was right.

I grunted and nodded a little, then started across the field between the farmhouse and the larger home at a fast walk. The tall grass had collected dew in the early morning hours, and it left damp tracks across my jeans.

I ignored the cold dampness and focused on my next steps. I'd take Chip home so he was there in time to get the kids ready for school. Warren was there making sure they were safe while we were out. Then I'd get with the investigator and see if we could find out where the necromancer went next. The hunt was on, and I was excited.

It was all just a normal night out for a Fae warrior princess.

2

Chip

Rose dropped me off at the house at a little after five in the morning. I took care to be quiet while coming inside. I didn't want to wake the kids. They didn't need to see me covered in zombie gore like I was. Despite being quiet, Warren, with his super werewolf hearing, knew I'd come home. He met me in the kitchen.

"Hmph, you look rough, dude. Did you catch the guy?"

"No, but I did manage to get way too close to a bunch of zombies."

"I know." Warren waved a hand in front of his nose. "I can smell it all over you. You need to get cleaned up before the kids wake up."

"My thoughts exactly. Thanks for holding down the fort."

Warren picked up his jacket and keys from the table in the dining room. "No problem. They never woke up, so I don't think they even knew I was here."

"Good, I don't like them to worry when Rose takes me out late at night on these little training missions."

"It's good for you to encounter different things in the Unusual world. I guess she should have warned you about necromancers and the zombies they create."

I shook my head. "No, I'm a big boy. I knew what we were walking into. Still, until you've faced a ravenous zombie trying to eat your brains, it's hard to understand the specific challenges involved in fighting them."

Warren chuckled and walked to the front door. I followed him, shaking his hand before he left. I watched him walk across the lawn to his SUV and then closed the door, turning the deadbolt and resetting the chain lock.

"Did you get the bad guy, Uncle Chip?"

I spun around to find Sadie standing on the landing of the stairs up to the bedrooms. I hoped she couldn't see the gore covering me in the early morning gloom with most of the lights off, but I knew there was little hope of that. Her enhanced Fae vision saw nearly as well in total darkness as in daylight.

"Um, no, but we did stop him from completing his plans."

Her nine-year-old eyes peered through the darkness at me, and she shook her head. "Aunt Rose says if you get the other guy's blood on you instead of your own, you're doing things right. I guess that means you won. Can I have breakfast?"

I fought down my worry of the gore coating me and said, "Sure, get a toaster pastry out of the freezer. You can make it yourself. I'm going to go wash up. As soon as I'm finished, I'll come back down so we can talk about all this."

She shrugged and walked down the rest of the steps and turned towards the kitchen. I watched her go and then hurried upstairs before Addy woke up. At five, he might have a much different reaction to all the blood and guts than his older sister did. Then again, he'd started training with Aunt Rose, too, so maybe not.

I stripped and immediately decided to write off the whole outfit. The jeans, T-shirt, jacket, and sneakers all had to go. I didn't want to run zombie brains and guts through my clothes washer. I was sure I'd never get the stink out if I did, no matter what the detergent brand said about stain mastery and odor control. I pulled a plastic trash bag from beneath the sink and stuffed the entire outfit inside.

The shower's powerful water jets felt good, though it stung at first as I washed and scrubbed at the caked-on gore on my exposed skin. There were more than a few scrapes and cuts hidden underneath I'd never noticed getting during the fight. Some had cut through my jacket's sleeves and pants, too. I'd make sure to put antibiotic ointment on them before I got dressed. Rose had assured me my Guardian magic would protect me from most magical effects from Unusual bites and such, but that didn't help with random germs that had to exist on a dead and decaying body.

After I swabbed and bandaged things as best I could, I got dressed. It was after six and it had taken me longer to get cleaned up than I expected. I snagged the plastic garbage bag with my soiled clothing and headed downstairs.

Sadie sat reading a book at the kitchen counter. She was on one of the barstools at the island. Bernard, the bed troll, sat on the stool next to her eating a bowl of cereal.

She looked up when I walked in and noticed the bag I carried right away. "You're throwing out the clothes you were wearing? I guess that's the right thing. They were pretty gross." She wrinkled up her nose as she said it.

"Yeah, no sense cleaning up that mess. What's your book about?" I leaned out the doorway into the garage and dropped the bag into the large rolling trash bin there.

"It's one Astrid gave me. A girl meets a boy at the beach, and they fall in love."

That caught me by surprise. She usually liked fantasy epics with swords and warrior princesses. I covered my shock by asking, "How is it?"

"It's okay. It's pretty unrealistic. I don't see how any girl would just fall in love with a guy like that in just a few days."

"Yeah, stuff like that never happens." I breathed a sigh of relief. I wasn't ready for the whole dating thing yet. "What are you going to say to Astrid?"

"I don't know yet. I think I'll keep reading before I decide. Maybe something later in the book will change my mind about it."

I loved that she read as much as she did, and I didn't care much about what genres she read as long as they weren't too adult in their themes. It was a great habit to have. When she didn't have homework or soccer practice, she could usually be found sitting somewhere reading.

Bernard looked up with a mouth full of crunchy wheat cereal. "Rose should have warned you about the possibility of zombies. You could have worn a pair of old coveralls or something disposable."

An image popped into my head of myself in a yellow hazmat suit and hood trying to fight off zombies with my sword. I decided it was a moot point. We weren't going back to that house and Rose had said the local Unusual community had a crew that would clean up the zombie infestation there.

"It's a shame the necromancer raised them to be ravenous killers," Bernard said, continuing his thought. "Most zombies I know are pretty decent folks."

That surprised me. "Know a lot of zombies, do you?"

"A few over the years. There's a pretty active ultimate frisbee league for zombies that runs across the state. I've been to a few of their matches in between assignments to kids like Sadie here. It's pretty exciting, especially with all the limbs and other bits falling off the players during the matches."

"You're kidding, right?" I'd heard and learned a lot about the Unusuals in the world, but this stretched credibility, even from what I knew.

Bernard held up his right hand. "Swear to the gods. Of course, they only play at night in the dark. Can't have humans witnessing that kind of carnage at a sporting event. They'd freak out."

"What happens when someone's leg falls off?" Sadie asked.

"They usually just reattach it somehow. I saw one guy get his arm reattached with a pneumatic nail gun on the spot. He went back in and started playing again right away."

"Cool," Sadie said. "I wish I'd seen that. My soccer games are so ordinary."

I corrected her, saying, "Ordinary is perfectly fine, Sadie. The extraordinary draws attention to us."

"Yeah, I know. We need to stay in hiding until I'm older. I remember the rules, Uncle Chip. It's just so hard to keep my strength and abilities to myself. I wish I were like the girls in one of my fantasy books. Then I could kick butt and take names the way I want to."

This had been coming up a lot lately. She wasn't really rebelling. Rose made sure to give her plenty of opportunities to use her burgeoning power during their sparring matches. That seemed to keep her desire to use her abilities in check for the most part.

"Sadie, honey, you have to remember it's not just about hiding who you are. It's also about not hurting your teammates or opponents when you're playing. Your magic is pretty wild right now. Aunt Rose says it'll settle down eventually, but until then, you have to keep yourself under control."

"Yeah, I guess so." Her lip pushed out in a little pout.

I smiled when I saw it. I'd heard that worked on softening up other dads with their daughters. I'd found I was mostly impervious to her cute little attempts at manipulation. It was quite the pout, though. It would have had most dads wrapped around their little girls' fingers. It was probably because I was home with the kids all the time. I'd become immune to these little tricks as I had watched her develop them over time.

"Are you finished eating?" I asked.

"Uh-huh."

"Come help me make lunch for you and Addy. Go and get the sandwich stuff from the fridge."

"Okay, Uncle Chip." She closed her book and hopped down off the stool.

"Hey, Sadie," I said while she dug in the refrigerator. "Where do zombie generals keep their armies?"

She rolled her eyes right on cue, knowing a dad joke was coming. "Where, Uncle Chip?"

"In their sleevies." I laughed. "Pretty good, huh?"

She tried not to smile as she brought back the lunch fixings.

We had almost finished making lunch when Addy came downstairs and joined us for his breakfast. I got him a toaster pastry and a banana, then poured him a glass of milk.

Bernard had quietly disappeared upstairs when he was finished eating to get some sleep in whatever dimension he disappeared into during the day. Addy's bed troll, Brunna, showed up though. She didn't say anything, as was usual. She just waved, grunted, and grabbed a banana from the bowl before returning up to Addy's room for her own rest time.

"Hey, buddy. Your sister and I are just about finished up with packing your lunch. Do you want chips or crackers to go with your sandwich?"

"Chips," he said around a mouthful of banana. Addy swallowed the food in his mouth and asked, "Did you and Aunt Rose go get a bad guy last night?" He pointed at the scratches and cuts on my arm.

I should have worn a long sleeve sweatshirt. The kids were getting too old and too smart to not notice battle damage when they saw it.

"We chased him off, yes. Warren came over to stay here, though, so you weren't alone at night. Okay?"

Addy's eyes brightened. "Is Uncle Warren still here?" He twisted in his seat to look through the open door into the dining room.

"No, he went home to sleep."

Warren had a trick he played with Addy where the werewolf would pretend to get angry about something silly and pop out his claws on one hand a finger at a time. Addy had thought that was hilarious since he was a toddler.

Addy deflated a little at the news the werewolf had already left.

"Don't worry, buddy. We can have him over soon for a cookout around the fire pit in the back yard. Does that sound like fun?"

Sadie perked up at the news we might have company over. "Can I invite Astrid? You could have Miss Patty over, too."

I hid a wince at the mention of Patty Peyton. She'd reverted to her maiden name since her divorce became final. The two of us had an on again, off again thing that was currently in the off phase. I know Sadie and Astrid were currently scheming to get us back together in true Parent Trap fashion, but I thought it was over for real this time. Patty had started to ask questions about things regarding Sadie's growing abilities that could lead to me revealing her destiny as the future Fae Queen. I liked Patty a lot, but not enough to give up that particular secret.

"I'm fine with Astrid coming over. We can do a sleep over if you want, but I'm sure Miss Patty will have something else to do."

"That means you aren't going to invite her, Uncle Chip." Sadie fixed me with a level stare. "I speak grown-up, you know."

I laughed. "Grown-up speak understand, do you?" I said in my mock Yoda voice.

Both kids smiled. They loved when I did my funny voices. I switched back to my normal voice. "Finish up and get dressed for school. It'll be time to leave before you know it."

I watched them while I cleaned up the lunch fixings and put everything away. Addy went back to his cereal and apple slices. Sadie returned to her book while her brother ate. When he finished his breakfast, they both left to go up and get dressed.

The grandfather clock by the front door chimed. We had to leave to walk down to the bus stop soon. The two of them were growing up faster than I realized sometimes. It worried me on some levels because there was so much they had to learn to fulfill their destinies. Sadie would become the first Fae Queen in over five hundred years and Addy must take up his role as her official champion. Their Aunt Rose and I had a lot of work to do before then.

3

Rose

The alarm on my phone went off, blaring Van Halen's *Right Now* from my nightstand. I groaned and rolled over. The night chasing the necromancer and fighting off his little zombie horde had taken more out of me than I liked to admit. I wondered if Chip was feeling the aches as much as I was.

I sat up and tapped the phone to stop the song. It was a great tune, but I'd had enough noise for now. It was early afternoon and I had to get ready to pick up Sadie and Addy at school. I took them to the dojo to train in weapons on Tuesdays and Thursdays. We'd started with quarterstaff work over the summer, and they had learned that style quickly. On Tuesday, I'd started in with simple bladed weapons. Both kids had been excited to move on to them and I knew they'd be ready for more of the same today.

I made a quick pass with a brush to help pull my hair back into a ponytail which I tied off with a leather thong, the way I'd been taught early in my own weapons training. I don't know why I'd never progressed to using a simple elastic band like everyone else. I think it was the habit and old-world connection it gave me. Tying my hair with a thong of rawhide was a way of paying homage to my predecessors, the Fae warrior princesses of long ago.

The phone buzzed with a notification, and I picked it up. It reminded me of Sadie's fourth grade field trip to Annapolis, the state capital of Maryland. She'd specifically asked if both Chip and I would join her on the trip as chaperones. I'd agreed, albeit reluctantly. I didn't mind Sadie and Addy at all, but their classmates could be a little rambunctious, and Sadie's best friend, Astrid, was a bit too much like her mother for my tastes.

One swipe took care of the notification. I'd have plenty of time to prepare for that adventure to the capital over the next week. Today, I had kids to train. Chip thought I was too tough on them in the sessions at the rented dojo space. I didn't see it that way. You trained the way you fought so you were ready for real battles. I did the same thing with Chip in his sparring matches with me. They all had a lot to learn before I exhausted what knowledge and skill I had to impart.

I sent Chip a reminder text message to pick up the kids after their training at the dojo and left to get Sadie and Addy. They loved when I picked them up in my restored candy apple red Firebird. The sports car stood out among the minivans and SUVs in the elementary school pick-up line. Sadi especially liked that she got to sit up front with me. Chip made them both sit in the back of the minivan due to the front airbags in the newer car. Neither of them was tall enough to sit up front there yet, but in the Firebird the rules were different. It was made before airbags were a thing.

Fifteen minutes later, I pulled into the school parking lot and drove over to the pick-up lane to get Sadie and Addy. The teacher's aide came around with her clipboard to check IDs and check off the kids that were getting picked up that day. My niece and nephew knew not to get on the bus on Tuesdays and Thursdays, but the school had their formalities. Schools were so much more locked down these days compared to when I was a kid. I would have been expected to figure it out on my own at this age.

Soon the bell rang, and the kids filed out the side door to their respective rides. Addy ran over first and popped open the passenger door. "Can I sit up front, Aunt Rose?"

"You know the rules, kiddo. Get in your booster in the back." I hooked a thumb over my shoulder.

Addy let out a sigh of resignation and flipped the seat forward to climb into the small back seat. He buckled in and waited for Sadie. It didn't take long. She bounced out with Astrid and a few other friends.

I checked the rear-view mirror. If Astrid was here, Patty probably was back in the line of cars behind me. I didn't know why my old high school nemesis still got under my skin. She was pleasant enough as an adult. It still bothered me that her daughter and Sadie were best friends. That forced us together from time to time during social events creating an awkwardness I'd rather have avoided. At least she and Chip weren't currently dating. They were positively disgusting when they were together. I bit back the hint of jealousy at the back of my mind. There was no chance for Chip and me to ever be more than co-parents to these two kids.

Sadie pulled the door open and flopped down in the passenger seat. She set her backpack on the floor between her feet and buckled in before closing the door. Once she was set, I pulled away into the slow-moving line of cars exiting the school lot onto the main road. I wanted to get away before the school buses did. It took forever to get anywhere once you were behind a school bus on its route to unload.

"Who wants to tell me about their day first?" When neither volunteered anything, I prompted them. "Addy, what was the favorite thing you did in school today?"

"Recess."

It was his usual answer. "What games did you play with your friends?"

He brightened at the thought of his school friends. "We pretended we were knights of the realm defending against a dragon. We pretended Mattie Long was the dragon."

Alarm bells sounded in my mind. "Addy, was she playing along, or were you playing that game without her permission?" Matilda was the daughter of a local witch coven leader. We didn't need a problem with her and her fellow witches. It was important for our family to maintain positive relationships with the various leaders in the Unusual community. Sadie might need to rely on them someday.

"It was Mattie's idea. She's faster than all of us boys and we couldn't catch her. It was still fun chasing after her."

I relaxed a little. Addy wasn't mean-spirited, but sometimes kids crossed over lines, and it was part of my job to make sure they knew they were to protect others, not victimize them.

"What about you, Sadie?" I asked. "What was your favorite part of the day?"

"In library time, I got to sit with Astrid and talk about the book we're reading together."

"Ewwww," Addy said. "You told me about that book. It has kissy stuff in it."

I smiled. Fourth grade was a little young for that, but Sadie and Astrid were Fae and they matured a little faster than human kids. It wasn't out of the realm of possibility that she was interested in having a special friend of some sort soon. I wondered if Chip knew about this. If he did, he was probably freaking out. That man was definitely going to be the overbearing parent type when it came to Sadie and future relationships. I wasn't. I was teaching her to defend herself. She wouldn't get into a situation with a significant other where she couldn't use her growing martial arts skills, or her innate magic to get out of.

"Books like that are fun, kiddo. If you have questions in there you don't want to ask Uncle Chip, you can always come to me. You know that, right? In fact, maybe we need to have another girl-to-girl chat about growing up."

Sadie rolled her eyes. "Astrid already had the talk with her mom. I heard about it from her. It's all pretty gross if what she says is true. I'm only reading the book because she suggested it." Her disgusted expression amused me even more. I knew that would all change soon enough. For now, though, I'd let her be a kid at heart. I wasn't going to hurry her into young adulthood.

We continued chatting about their school day, now that I'd broken the ice and gotten them talking. Before I knew it, we had pulled into the parking lot at the strip mall with the dojo space I rented. The sensei who owned it cleared his class calendar so I could train the kids alone without prying eyes watching what I taught them. Using their Fae magical talents in tandem with their weapons was something that only came with constant practice. If it was to be practical, it had to become second nature and part of their muscle memory.

Once inside the dojo, the kids set their backpacks against the wall. They each started stretching the way I'd taught them to. Good training habits led to stronger and more rapid growth in the different forms I worked on with them. I stood waiting in the center of the room with their wooden practice blades in one hand and my own in the other.

"Swords again, cool!" Addy exclaimed. "I got tired of that staff stuff. You can't stab someone with a quarterstaff or chop off their head." He slashed at the air with an imaginary sword.

"Don't denigrate someone with a staff, Addy." I tucked my wooden blade under my other arm and tapped the side of my head. "The weapon is up here. These are just tools for a job that needs doing. It's the person that is deadly. Don't forget that. I once had to kill a vampire and all I had was a number two pencil."

"Nuh-uh," Sadie said. "There's no way, even for you, Aunt Rose."

I held up my right hand. "I swear to the gods. Let me tell you, I had a heck of a time pushing that thing all the way into his heart." I didn't tell them the rogue vamp had already been sorely weakened because I'd flung it out through a window into the afternoon sunlight. But they didn't need to know all the details of that particular fight. Most of the blood suckers were perfectly decent, even if they were overly proud people.

I handed their practice blades to them and held out my own in front of me in a ready stance. "Let's go through the forms to practice all the attack positions and the respective defensive shifts from each of them."

"Can't we just spar?" Sadie asked. "The forms are boring."

"You can't spar if you don't know the ways you can use the blade. The training forms teach them to you. Now, swords up. Follow along with me."

We worked on their forms for a good half hour until they each could follow me without mistakes. Then I transitioned to other work. Addy was a little young for the next part, so I gave him my tablet to sit on the side and play a game while I worked with Sadie. She was old enough to start trying simple, very basic spells, called cants. If she mastered them, she could work them into her training katas with her blade.

The first thing I wanted to teach her was a simple pull. It was often used to summon small objects to a spell caster's hand. In combat, though, I'd found it was sometimes just enough to tip a person off-balance when they lunged or extended themselves in some other way.

"Sadie, hold out your hand, palm up, towards the metal trash can over there. Now focus your attention on it and curl pointer and middle fingers back toward you in a quick gesture of summoning."

"Aunt Rose, I can't just summon a trash can to come here."

I put my hands on my hips. "How do you know? Have you already tried this?"

"No, but I don't have that kind of power."

"You're only right if you don't try. Now hand up and focus. Think about the trash can coming toward you."

She frowned and faced the trash can with her hand reaching out in its direction. She curled her fingers back slowly.

"Move your fingers faster. You're calling it to come to you. Use your fingers to tell it what to do."

She repeated the move faster a few times and then lowered her arm. "See, I told you. It won't work. I don't have that kind of magic. The only thing I can do is see who people are inside."

"That's a different part of your inner self. This is Fae magic that everyone in our family has. Now hand up. Try again. We're going to keep at this until you get it to move."

She tried again and again, getting more and more frustrated.

I forced her to keep going. This was going to take some sort of breakthrough and it wouldn't come easily.

Finally, she stomped her foot when I repeated the word, "Again."

Sadie whirled around to face me, her eyes cold and hard with anger.

I didn't flinch. I nodded at the trash can and said, "Again."

She huffed and spun around as she lifted her hand in a quick flowing motion. The two fingers beckoned to the can. To her surprise, it slid a few feet across the wooden floor in her direction.

Sadie's eyes lit up with delight. "I did it. I did it. Aunt Rose, did you see that?"

"I did. Now do it again. Once you can do it every time, I'll show you how it works in a fight."

That prospect excited her and she worked hard for the next half hour until she could do it every time. The small waste bucket didn't weigh much, so it didn't take too much mana to make the spell work. It would take a lot more to move a person.

"Okay, now come over here and stand across from me. I'm going to lunge at you with my blade. You already know the counter to that. Parry my blade and while you do, extend the other arm and use the pull cant on me."

"But you're too big, Aunt Rose."

"I am, but it's about leverage. When someone is tipped forward in a lunge or other extension attack, it doesn't take much to pull them off-balance. Now, sword up."

I squared off opposite my niece and waited until her sword came up. Then I lunged in, trying to slip past her guard. I didn't want to injure her, just get close enough to prove my point.

On the first attempt her timing was off, and she missed with both the parry and the spell. I gave her a painful tap on her knee with the flat of my practice sword.

"Ow. What was that for?"

"To teach you to keep your guard up. I made that lunge easy to block and you still missed. Try again."

Sadie raised her blade to the ready position. I turned in place and lunged in at her as I came around.

This time, her sword came around and clacked against mine to knock it aside so it passed beside her waist. At the same moment, her left hand swept up and two fingers gestured at me.

It was my turn to be surprised. I'd expected a small tug and was ready to resist it. It was more a forceful yank against my chest, and I stumbled forward a few steps until I caught my balance.

Sadie laughed and jumped up and down. "Aunt Rose, I did it. You really almost fell."

"Yes, I did. You are more powerful than you think, Sadie. Don't ever forget that. You have magic in your blood. It's coursing through you all the time. When you need it, it's there for you to call upon."

She smiled and whirled in place until she suddenly stopped, facing the trash can. This time, when she beckoned, it slid all the way across the floor to stop at her feet.

I didn't expect her to progress this quickly with this particular skill, but I was happy to see it. It meant I could start advancing her to other attack and spell combinations.

Through the window in the dojo's front door, I spotted Chip pull up in the minivan. "Okay, that's enough for today. You still have to go home and do your homework. Your uncle's here. Let's pack up and do our final stretches. That means you, too, Addy. Put the tablet away in my purse and come over to finish with Sadie and me."

This had been one of our more productive sessions and I was excited about what it meant for Sadie's continued training. As she grew older, she'd be in situations where she'd be on her own more and more often. I wanted her to have all the skills to protect herself I could impart. I would make sure this particular Fae Queen ascended her throne.

4

Chip

Saturday rolled around and I stood at the island in the kitchen prepping orange slices for both kids' soccer games later that day. It was my week to bring the fruit for the teams. Other parents would fill up and bring the big orange water cooler, along with other snacks for after the day's matches.

Addy and Sadie had both exhibited the quick and nimble footwork that made a child perfect for this sport. While I had grown up playing football most of my life and graduated high school as the star quarterback, I appreciated the other sports my classmates had played. Soccer had always intrigued me, and I marveled at the ball control my friends had shown using just their feet.

Now I was the parent of two talented soccer players. Some of it was undoubtedly their Fae abilities, but I was certain a big portion of it came from the Proctor side of the family. Though their father, Bobby, hadn't been the star I had been in later years, he'd been quite the athlete in his younger days.

Addy walked into the kitchen, his cleats already on his feet. I glanced down and frowned. He'd left clumps of dried mud all across the floor. He obviously hadn't cleaned off his cleats after his last game like he was supposed to. "Take those off and go get the broom, Addison Proctor. You know better than to put those on in the house."

He stopped and looked behind him and then down at his shoes. "Awww, Uncle Chip, I like the sound they make on the hard floors when I walk. Plus, they make me taller."

"I don't care. Take them off now. And clean up this mess."

Sadie looked up from her book where she sat at the kitchen table. "Addy's in trou-ble." She drew out the last word, mocking her chastised brother.

"Just for that, Sadie, you can get the dustpan and help him. He made a mistake. That isn't reason to make fun of him. I don't let him do that to you when you get corrected."

"Uncle Chip," she said. "That's not fair."

"We're a family. We help each other all the time. That's our rule. Now get up or I'll take your book away for the rest of the day."

She huffed and closed the book. She went into the garage with Addy and came back with the dustpan to hold while Addy handled the broom. It took the five-year-old a little time to complete the clean-up, which annoyed Sadie even more. But she wisely kept her annoyance in check and even encouraged him a few times with suggestions that helped him with the oversized-for-his-hands kitchen broom.

"Good," I said. "Now get the rest of your gear packed up. We're leaving for the rec league field complex in fifteen minutes."

While the kids got their extra clothes and clean socks packed up in their duffle bags, I finished bagging up the orange slices. They both came down in their uniform jerseys. Addy's team was sponsored by a pizza place in town that had been there when I was a kid growing up. Sadie's team was sponsored by a local plumber. The businesses paid for the jerseys for their teams and helped cover the cost of field maintenance and other expenses to run the leagues each year.

We loaded up in the van and headed across town to the rec center where there were a half-dozen soccer fields in one centralized location. There were also walking trails, playground equipment for kids not participating in the matches, and even a half dozen pickleball courts. Those courts were surprisingly popular and at least one was in use every time I was there.

The kids' games overlapped a little, so Rose was supposed to meet me before Addy's team started playing. She was usually there to watch them play, but today, I would need her there to stay with Addy while I walked over and watched Sadie's game begin. I spotted the red Firebird in one of the parking spots in the far corner of the lot. I scanned the crowded fields nearby to see if I could spot her.

"Looking for me?"

The voice right behind me caused me to jump and turn around. "Rose, stop sneaking up on me like that. I get it. You're a super-stealthy warrior princess."

"The point is to get to where I don't surprise you, Chip. You're supposed to expect the unexpected. That's the whole point of all of our training."

"My Guardian skills and abilities alert me when there's real danger to the kids. You aren't a threat to them, so I don't pick up on you sneaking up on me. You're a loophole in the whole process."

Rose put her hands on her hips and assumed that know-it-all look she got. "There are bad guys out there who can mask their intentions. That could spoof your abilities. Don't become complacent. You need to always be on your guard."

I resisted the urge to snap off a curt answer. We didn't need to be fighting here in public. Sadie and Addy had to get to their teams. "You're right, Rose. I'll work harder. For now, though, the kids have games to play. You take Addy over to his team. They're on field number three. I'll walk Sadie over to number five to join her team, then come back for the start of Addy's match."

"I can walk over there by myself, Uncle Chip. I'm big enough to carry my bag and find the coach." Sadie had pulled her soccer backpack on her shoulders and looked up at me with a hopeful expression.

Her request tempted me for just a moment and then I remembered Rose was here. "No, I'll walk with you. I know you're growing up fast but humor your old uncle for now."

Rose gave a slight nod of approval and reached down for Addy's hand. "Come on, kiddo. Let's go and find your team."

Addy waddled along beside his aunt under the weight of his own backpack. He insisted on carrying it himself, though. Anything Sadie could do, he tried to do as well. It was usually harmless and kind of cute how he looked up to his big sister.

Sadie bounced on the balls of her feet beside me, not bothering to hide her impatience.

"All right, I see you waiting. Let's go and find your field and get you started warming up."

Sadie skipped along beside me as I took long strides towards the far side of the complex. Her coach was the father of one of Sadie's teammates, Joanie. She ran up to him, waving as she approached.

"Hi, Mr. Simpson."

"Hiya, Sadie. Ready for a fun time?"

"You bet. We're going to win for sure this morning."

I caught up and smiled. "As long as you and the others try your hardest, that's what counts." I nodded at the coach. "Hey, Sam. How're ya doing?"

"Fair to middling. I can't complain and, hey, I get to coach these fine young ladies each week."

I couldn't tell if he was being sarcastic or serious. He always had a smile on his face, so it was hard to say. I smiled and nodded, not knowing how else to respond.

Holding up the bag of orange sections, I looked around. "Where do you want me to put these?"

"Over by the orange water cooler is fine. Someone's supposed to show up with a separate cooler full of ice. We'll put them in there when they get here." Sam pointed at the field. "Sadie, why don't you grab a ball and start on some dribbling and passing drills just like we did in practice this week."

Sadie ran to get one of the balls out of the nylon ball bag nearby. She dropped it on the ground and ran out onto the pitch, keeping the ball just in front of her. She was nimble anyway, and that lent to her footwork as she worked with the soccer ball. It was impressive to watch.

Several of the other girls, including Joanie, ran out to join her. I spotted Astrid in the mix and scanned the crowd until I found Patty talking with a few of the other mothers nearby. I left Sam to his coaching duties and walked over to join them.

"Hey, Chip," one of the moms, Grace, said as I approached.

"Hello, ladies. Are we ready for a fun-filled morning of soccer?"

They all laughed. Patty met my eyes as she joined in the laughter. There was a little sparkle in them as always. I smiled back at her. We'd ended our last couple of dates on good terms and I was glad to see we could still be friends.

"I'm here to drop off the oranges before the game. I have to head over to Addy's game which starts in a few minutes."

Patty held out her hand. "Give the bag to me. I'll hold onto them until Melvin Crow gets here with the ice and cooler."

"Thanks, that's a big help."

Grace asked, "You will be back for the girls' match, won't you?"

"Yes, Sadie's aunt is over with Addison. I'll come back before the action starts."

"Good," she said. "We'll need all the cheering we can get. This team today is going to be tough to beat. They're very good."

"The girls are up to it, I'm sure," I said. "They've looked good in practices, plus they won the last two games they played."

Patty shook her head. "The other team has won the championship for two years running."

"Then they're primed for defeat. Don't worry, I'll be back before you know it."

I waved to the ladies and left them to their conversation. I heard giggling a few seconds later and turned back to look their way. They were all looking at me. As soon as they saw me glancing back their way, they burst into gales of laughter. I didn't know what was so funny, but clearly, I was the butt of the joke. I'm sure it was something to do with Patty and me dating. She did like to gossip and enjoyed her girl-talk.

Addy's game was getting ready to start when I arrived back at his field. I took my spot beside Rose and watched as the players took the field. At this age, the coaches were allowed on the field, too, to help direct the players and try to keep them in some semblance of position on the pitch. If they didn't, there'd just be a swarm of kids mobbing the ball.

I cheered them on while they chased the ball around the field. There were no goals, or even shots on goals while I was there, but the kids seemed to be having a great time and that was all that mattered at this age. I checked my watch and nudged Rose next to me with an elbow.

"Hey, I'm heading over to Sadie's game now. I'll see you there when you're finished here."

"Have fun. Don't make all the soccer moms swoon too much."

I rolled my eyes. "Seriously, Rose, they're very over me by now. Patty is with them and the last time I saw them, they were all sharing a laugh at my expense."

"Good, someone has to keep you humble." She followed it up with a smile of her own and turned back to cheer as Addy broke from the pack with the ball. It was only for a few seconds before the mob caught up to him, but it was exciting.

I left her to continue cheering for Addy and I headed across the complex to watch Sadie's game. It would be a more serious affair compared to the first graders. The competitive athlete inside me threatened to rise at moments like this, even though I tried to keep the focus on the kids. I didn't want to become one of those hyper-serious parents who forgot it was a game. There were a few of those around and they tended to make their kids miserable on and off the pitch. I wanted Sadie to play because she enjoyed the game, not because I was pushing her to succeed and be a certain kind of player. She'd have enough on her plate learning all she'd need to become the future queen. She didn't need an overbearing soccer uncle, too.

5

Rose

After Chip walked away, I paid more attention to the game. Addy's match ended in a tie, though I don't think anyone was keeping official score. It was more of a free-for-all chasing the ball around. I knew the result, though. Keeping score was important to me. If you didn't keep track, how could you know who won, whether in a game, or in life?

I waited while Addy and the other kids ate their way through the orange slices and water. It was a warm day for October and the kids were hot after chasing the ball around. I heard a cheer across the nearby fields and wondered if that had come from Sadie's game. I checked my watch and then walked over to fetch Addy from where he stood chatting with a few of his friends.

"Hey, Addy, it's time to go and watch your sister play."

"Do I have to?" His pleading whine grated on me a little, but I ignored it.

"Yes, you have to. Come on. I want to watch her play, too."

The kid's shoulders slumped, and he said goodbye to his team-mates. I waved over to the coach to signal I was taking Addy with me. He nodded and went back to talking to a few of the moms clustered around him. They were probably busting his chops for not playing their superstars enough.

We walked across the multi-field complex until we reached the pitch where Sadie had her match. The score cards at the officials' table showed a tie score of one to one. Chip stood near the players' bench watching from the sidelines. Addy and I joined him. Patty Peyton stood a few yards away with a couple of the other soccer moms. I glanced her way and then turned my back on her to talk to Chip.

"Oh, good, you're here." Chip said as he noticed me standing there. "Sadie just went in as a sub."

"The coach didn't start her? She's at least as good as any other player on the team."

Chip shook his head. "Remember this is rec league play, Rose. Everyone gets a chance to play and learn. Besides, she still ends up playing more of the game than most of her teammates."

Sadie ran past us and gave me a wave and a big grin. She veered into the path of another player from the opposite team and charged in the direction of the ball. The opposing player reached out and pushed her from the side instead of running into her.

Sadie's arms went wide, and she sprawled on the grass, landing hard. I looked at the teenager who was reffing the game. She'd been looking the other way and didn't see the foul.

I yelled, "Hey, Ref. Foul." I pointed at Sadie on the ground. She'd rolled over and had started to get up.

The ref watched as Sadie got up and shrugged. She returned her attention to the players around the ball as they advanced it down the field.

I glanced back at Sadie and drew in a sharp breath. Her sapphire blue eyes flared with power. Even in the bright sunlight, I caught the glint of it in her gaze.

"Uh-oh," I said.

"What? Is she hurt?" Chip asked. "She looks okay. See, she's getting up."

"Look at her eyes, Chip."

He stared at his niece for a second. "Oh, that's not good." He raised his voice. "It's okay, Sadie. Let it go and brush it off."

"You think that's enough to keep her temper in check." I looked around for the coach as I continued whispering to Chip. "She needs to come out of the game. She's drawn on the power within her. It's hard to let go once you do that, even as an adult. There's no telling what she'll do."

"She's a smart girl," Chip said. "She wouldn't dare expose herself that way. There are all these people around."

The hairs rose on my forearms along with the goosebumps that signaled someone had embraced natural magic nearby. Sadie ran towards the action and the girl who'd pushed her down.

That other young player had the ball, and she was good. She skillfully wove in and around the other players as she drove towards the opposing goal.

Sadie came in like a bullet from the side. She reached out with her right hand and beckoned at the running player with two fingers.

With a yelp of surprise, the girl spilled over forward and sprawled on the grass. She landed hard and rolled over a few times before she came to a stop.

Sadie swooped in and took the ball, running back up the field. She moved with unnatural grace and speed as she evaded all the other team's players. Every time a player came her way, the first two fingers on her right hand twitched and the ball swerved around them, letting Sadie drive forward in an almost straight line. She'd obviously taught herself the opposite of pull and learned to push, too.

A tug on my elbow spun me around.

Patty Peyton, whose Fae senses had also alerted her to magic use on the pitch, came right up in my face, her voice hissing in a harsh whisper. "Stop her, Rose. You see what she's doing. Someone is going to notice something weird is going on."

"What do you want me to do, Patty, run out and tackle her? I see it, too, and I plan on dealing with her breach in protocol as soon as she comes out of the game."

I twisted back around just in time to see Sadie kick the ball at the goal from twenty yards out. The goalie dove for it and should have had it, but the ball juked at the last instant and sped past her reaching hands.

A cheer went up from the assembled parents and spectators on our side of the field as the ball bounced into the back of the net. Sadie's teammates all ran up to her and congratulated her on the goal.

It was time to put an end to this. I left Patty and Chip and walked over to the coach who was calling instructions for his players to reset and continue the game.

"Coach, please take Sadie Proctor out of the game. There's a family matter we have to attend to."

He glanced my way and then back at the field. "Are you kidding? Were you watching what she did? We need her to stay in there and rally the team to hold onto this win."

Chip had joined me beside the coach. He said, "Rose is right. It's time for Sadie to go home. I forgot to tell you before the match that there was a prior engagement for the family today."

The coach didn't bother to hide his annoyance. His scowl showed it all as he waved to one of the other players. "Jenny, you go in for Sadie Proctor. She has to go home."

"Yes, Coach."

The selected girl ran out onto the field and tapped Sadie on the shoulder. Sadie's eyes still gleamed as she turned to face the other girl. I raised my hand to get her attention and waved for her to come off the field.

Sadie stormed off the field as the ref reset the ball at midfield to restart. She didn't come to us, instead going straight to her backpack. She lifted it onto her shoulders, settled it into place, and walked past us in silence towards the parking lot.

"What do we do?" Chip said. "That certainly can't happen again."

"I'll deal with Sadie. You grab Addy and meet me back at home."

Chip hesitated for a second about ceding authority to me on this, then he nodded. "Addy, come over here. It's time to go home."

I left it to him to collect the boy. I had to go and catch up to Sadie. She was almost to the parking lot. I jogged after her and caught up to her near the minivan.

"Sadie, you're coming home with me. I'm parked over there." I pointed across the lot to the far side where my Firebird was parked.

She spun around on me. Her eyes flared with power. "Maybe I

don't want to go home with you, Aunt Rose. You're just going to yell at me."

"You bet I'm going to yell at you, Sadie." I lowered my voice before continuing. "But I'm not going to do it here in the middle of a mundane parking lot where any random human idiot can overhear us."

Sadie stomped her foot and glared at me for a second, then let out an exasperated groan and stalked off towards my car. I hid a smile behind my hand with a feigned cough. Those theatrics were new, and I realized this might be a precursor of what was to come from her in a few years. I wasn't looking forward to that time yet. I remember dealing with Aunt Allura at the time when I was an early teenager. She'd taken over watching Lili and me after our parents died. It was not the fondest of my childhood memories.

I walked over to where Sadie stood with her arms crossed beside the Firebird. I used the key to unlock her door and then walked around to my side. She tossed her backpack into the back and flopped down in the passenger seat. I started the car and drove out of the lot. I decided to take a circuitous route back to their house.

Sadie noticed I hadn't turned the normal way home. "Where are we going?"

"We need some time to chat, just you and me. We haven't had the chance to do that in a while. Addy's always with us and there are some things we ladies need to talk about sometimes."

I could tell from the quizzical look on Sadie's face she was surprised by this approach. That was good. I didn't think straight out yelling was the best way to go. She was stubborn, like her mother, like me, and would just dig in her heels. I needed to finesse this so she realized on her own that she couldn't do this kind of thing in public again.

"You were lucky back there, you know that?"

"What do you mean?"

"It was a bright and sunny day. Most people will chalk up the light behind your eyes as a glint from the sunlight. If it had been cloudy or at night, people would have noticed something wasn't right about you."

Sadie flipped down the visor to check her face in the mirror.

"It's okay, now. Your magic has subsided."

"I-I forgot about that part when I did what I did."

"It was sloppy, Sadie." I glanced her way. "That's not like you. You let your guard down and gave in to the lure of easy power. The problem with that is using the magic too much can become a crutch and will ultimately draw the wrong kind of attention to you."

"What's the good of having all this power if I can't use it? All it does is make me a freak."

"You're only a freak if you let that label stick." I remembered my high school years when I basked in the light of being the freaky, goth younger sister of Lili the homecoming queen. "It's not something to aspire to, believe me."

"What do you know about that, Aunt Rose? You're an awesome warrior who fights real monsters with your magic all the time."

"Now, sure," I replied. "Back when I was your age, I acted weird on purpose, and I regretted it for a long time afterward. You see the way Miss Patty and I still act with each other. That dates back to when we were in school together. You don't want to hurt your relationship with Astrid, do you?"

"Why would what I did affect me and Astrid?"

"Think it through, Sadie. You're a smart girl. Astrid is Fae, just like you. If she keeps hanging around you and weird things keep happening, then others will wonder if she's like you, too."

Sadie's shoulders slumped a little. "Oh, I hadn't thought about that. Do you think she's angry with me?"

"No, but don't be surprised if her mother keeps her away from playing with you until she finds out how we handled what you did."

"That's not fair. Astrid didn't do anything."

I nodded. "Sometimes just being around the wrong person at the wrong time can rub off on you. Miss Patty's too smart to let that happen to Astrid. She'll end your play time with her daughter if she thinks you're a danger to her safety and the secret of her Unusual self."

We drove along in silence for a few minutes until we pulled up out in front of Sadie's house. I sat there with the motor running for a bit to let Sadie gather her thoughts.

After about a minute, I switched off the engine and asked, "Have you thought about what you're going to tell your uncle about what you did? He's going to want an explanation."

"I guess I'll tell him I'm sorry. But I just got so mad when that girl knocked me down. It wasn't fair."

I shook my head. "A real apology doesn't have the word 'but,' or an explanation. You're either sorry or there's a real reason that justifies what you did. There isn't any middle ground."

"But…"

I raised an eyebrow as soon as she said it.

A wry grin crossed Sadie's face. "Right. No excuses. Just say I'm sorry."

"Good." I opened my car door. "Let's go in and see if we can scrounge up something to eat. When you use up your mana like you did today, you need to refuel as soon as you can."

Together, we went up the front sidewalk and into the house. I thought I'd handled it well enough. I worried what this meant for the future for our girl, though. If she was anything like I was, I might not survive. The thought brought a wry chuckle from me. Aunt Allura had once warned me I would someday face someone just like my younger self. That prophecy had just come true.

6

Chip

The front door opened, and I looked up from where Addy and I sat in the family room watching a movie on the TV. It was Rose and Sadie. They'd taken a long way home and I'd had time to get Addy a quick bath to wash the dirt and grass stains off of him.

"You two came home by the scenic route I guess."

Rose gave Sadie a gentle nudge and my niece came over to where we sat.

"I'm sorry, Uncle Chip. I shouldn't have used my magic like that. It was cheating and I knew better."

She turned to look back at her aunt. Rose gave a slight nod and Sadie looked back to me. Her large eyes brimmed with tears. I was still angry at what she'd done, but clearly, she and Rose had come to some sort of understanding. I didn't want to upset any punishment Rose had put in place. I'd ask her about it later.

I held out my arms and Sadie melted into them, sobbing and saying, "I'm sorry," over and over again.

We hugged until she stopped crying. I let go and held her out at arm's length. "I don't expect to have this kind of conversation again. Do you understand?"

Sadie wiped at her eyes. "Yes, Uncle Chip."

"Good, now I'll bet you want some lunch. Why don't you go into the kitchen and make sandwiches for lunch with Addy. I had him wait until you got home."

She nodded. "Come on, Addy. I'll let you spread the peanut butter."

Addy jumped up with a little fist pump and ran after his sister into the kitchen.

I waited until the door swung closed and glanced at Rose. "Your ride together seemed to have worked out well enough."

Rose came over to sit on the easy chair next to the sofa. "She understands what she did was wrong and that there wasn't an excuse no matter how angry she was. That's the important part."

"What kind of punishment did you give her? I want to make sure we present a united front on this."

Rose shook her head. "No punishment. I just had a long talk about how disappointed we were in what she did."

"Rose, she needs to have some consequence for what she did out there. If one of those other girls had been seriously injured by her magic, it could have exposed all of us. You of all people should understand that. You lecture me often enough about it."

"I'm not going to be bad cop to your good cop, Chip. You're not going to make me the disciplinarian while we raise these kids. It's bad enough that I don't live here all the time. I won't be the bad guy who comes over and lays the hammer down, too. Besides, what kind of punishment did you have in mind? Should we ground her? I can guarantee Patty's not going to let Astrid come over and play anytime soon until she knows this is resolved."

"All the more reason we should do something. Patty will want to know how we handled it."

I knew that was the wrong thing to say as soon as it left my mouth.

Rose's eyebrows lowered and her eyes grew dark. "We're not raising these kids by committee with Patty Peyton, Chip. She doesn't get a say in this."

"No, of course not. But we have to do something. Maybe you should cut back on the magic instruction for the time being. She doesn't need to know any more little tricks she can let loose when she gets angry."

"That's not going to happen. If anything, this is a reason to increase her magical instruction time. We can't afford to have her stumbling around with that kind of power learning on her own. She needs direction and an outlet."

"But that sounds a lot like you're rewarding her, Rose." I didn't understand why she didn't see it the way I did. "You have to give her some consequence over this. She can't just skate away for free."

Rose sighed. "Look, let it rest for a day or two. I suspect there's going to be a reaction among her friends. The humans on that field couldn't detect the magic, but that doesn't mean they didn't see something happen that shouldn't have happened. They have a sort of sixth sense about staying away from magic, even if they don't understand why it makes them uncomfortable. Kids are especially sensitive to it. See what Sadie has to deal with at school before you decide on adding a consequence. If I'm wrong, we can come to a decision about it later. Fair enough?"

I thought about it. I hadn't considered how strange the whole scene on the soccer field looked to the uninitiated. If Rose was right, Sadie was going to have a rough time going back to school on Monday if word got out about something no one could explain about her. A lot of kids her age already had cell phones and text apps. Word would get around soon enough.

"That's fair." I paused in thought. "Do you really think she will encounter much trouble at school? Should we keep her home?"

"I don't think so. But we'll see. You could email her teacher and give her a heads up."

"But Mrs. Nelson is completely human. She won't understand."

Rose laughed. "Don't tell her everything, just say Sadie had something happen with some of her friends after the soccer game and could she keep an eye on the situation for you. Believe me, this isn't the first girl drama she's had to deal with in her career. She'll know what to do."

I wasn't sure about this, but I had to trust Rose about things like this. Boys and girls dealt with arguments and fights in very different ways. If she thought the teacher could help Sadie navigate what was coming at school in the next week, then I'd trust her instincts.

"I'll email her tonight before bed." I stood up and nodded to the kitchen. "Do you want lunch? I made some chicken salad yesterday. There's plenty if you want it."

"I'd like that," Rose said. She followed me into the kitchen.

The kids had made a bit of a mess getting lunch together. They had settled on having peanut butter sandwiches and some corn chips. Sadie had gotten them milk, and both sat at the counter on the tall stools while they ate.

"Gee, what happened?" I asked. "Did a peanut butter grenade go off in here?" There were smears of peanut butter on the counter, the refrigerator door handle, and up both of Addy's arms.

Addy laughed. "Good one, Uncle Chip."

"I'm glad you liked it. You're going to need another bath, though."

Addy shrugged and then paused to lick at the peanut butter on his forearm.

Sadie grimaced. "Ewww, boys are so gross."

"Try it, Sadie. It tastes good." He reached out to smear some of the peanut butter from the back of his hand on her arm.

She shrieked and hopped off her chair. She scooped up her plate and glass of milk and moved to the round table in the corner. "I'm sitting over here with the civilized people."

It was my turn to laugh. I loved these kids more than I could fathom sometimes. Even with what Sadie did earlier, I could never stay angry at either of them for long. My hand reached up and touched the gold shark's tooth on the chain around my neck. I could feel its outline beneath my T-shirt.

A moment of sadness came over me as I considered this another moment in time missed by my late brother. Bobby would have been so much better at this than I was. I always felt like I was stumbling along without a plan. Even with Rose's help, it was a lot of work raising these two kids.

"Hey, Chip, you going to get out that chicken salad or not? You promised me a sandwich."

Rose's words broke through my thoughts, and I blinked to clear my cloudy eyes. "Yeah, give me a second. You go and get the kaiser rolls I bought. They're in the bread box over there."

While she got the rolls, I got out the bowl of chicken salad, some mayo, and the salt and pepper. With the fixings all laid out, the two of us made our lunch and sat down with Sadie at the round table to eat. I had to stop halfway through my sandwich to help Addy wash up at the sink. He'd finished and wanted to go watch some TV, and I didn't want him smearing peanut butter all over the couch.

While I was at the sink with Addy, Rose asked, "When's that field trip I'm supposed to go on? It's coming up soon, isn't it?"

"Yes," I said. "The trip to Annapolis is in one week from this Monday. I hope you're still able to come. Mrs. Nelson stressed the need for a few extra chaperones."

"Yeah, I'll be there. I'm still not sure how we both got roped into going along on this trip."

I said, "There aren't a lot of parents home or available during the daytime for something like this. Besides, it might be fun. I remember a similar trip I went on when I was Sadie's age. My friends and I had a great time."

"I hope you're right. Spending the day traipsing around the state capital with a horde of children isn't my idea of fun."

Sadie said, "Aunt Rose, it'll be fun. Astrid and I have a whole plan. Mrs. Nelson gave us a map of the old part of the city with the capitol building and the governor's mansion. We want to try and see everything. It'll be so much fun."

"See, Rose. With an endorsement like that, how can it possibly go wrong?"

She fixed me with a level stare. "I'll let you know in a week."

7

Rose

I hadn't ridden on a school bus in at least fifteen years. Ten minutes into this bus ride, I was already regretting not driving the Firebird to Annapolis and meeting the field trip there.

"Why the frown, Rose?" Chip asked from his seat across the aisle at the front of the bus.

I put my hand down to shift my butt on the seat and immediately pulled it up again. "I'm too old to be riding a school bus. This seat is sticky. The kids are already too noisy. And did I mention I'm too old for this? I should have met you there and driven myself."

The instant chuckle from Chip added another down check to my list. He didn't get to be amused by my discomfort.

"You can't be a chaperone and not ride with the kids, Rose. That's not how that works. Besides, this is a great chance to get to see Sadie in a different setting."

I shifted my position sideways in the seat so I could see back there, too. Sadie sat in a window seat near the very back of the bus. Instead of chatting with the girls engaged in an animated discussion around her, she stared out the window. I realized she was alone in her seat, too, and the other kids were ignoring her, even Astrid, her best friend.

"I'm watching, Chip, but I'm not liking what I'm seeing."

He glanced back and a frown replaced his smile. "I was hoping the trip away from school would be better. She said something last night about Astrid not talking to her, but I figured her other friends were treating her normally."

"I was afraid of this," I said. I scooted over and joined Chip in his seat so we could talk without being overheard by the other two moms sitting close by. "I wonder if Astrid was told to avoid Sadie for a while and the other kids saw her reaction and followed her lead after what happened at the soccer game. I think the other kids have labeled her as weird and are pushing her away."

Chip craned his neck to look back at Sadie. "What do we do? Aside from mentioning Astrid, she didn't tell me about any of this."

"We do nothing," I said with a shrug. "I told you there'd be consequences. Hopefully, the other kids forget about it, and they all let her back into the group. It's hit or miss at this age. If she were Addy's age, it would be almost certain that it would pass. But at this age, there's the penchant for cliques and the whole mean girl thing is starting to rear its ugly head."

"Maybe we can give her an important job to do with our group while we tour the capital?" Chip's hopeful expression indicated his idea might solve this problem.

"I'm not sure, Chip. We'll have to see what happens when we get there and start the tour. Kids can be cruel in the same way they can be totally open and accepting. Their emotions and understanding of the world are much more black and white that ours is."

I slid back over to my slightly sticky seat and settled in for the remainder of the hour and a half drive to the capital. I was pretty sure Sadie would find a way through this on her own. That didn't mean I wouldn't keep an eye on her. There wasn't much I could do to fix it. I considered having a chat with Patty the next time I saw her. We usually avoided contact with each other, but if she'd initiated this ostracism through Astrid then I needed to deal with it. Maybe I could find a way to convince her to lift whatever instructions she'd given her daughter.

I tuned out the chatter and settled back in the seat while I watched the world pass by outside the bus. I must have dozed off, because the next thing I knew, Chip tapped me on the shoulder.

"Hey, we're here. Time to earn our keep."

I sat up and arched my back to work out the kinks from falling asleep in an awkward position. I stood and got off the bus with Chip. Before we left, we had been assigned a group of ten kids, including Sadie. We were responsible for keeping track of them, making sure they were on schedule, and getting them back to the bus before it was time to leave.

As we stepped off the bus, the teacher, Mrs. Nelson, who'd been riding on the other bus, handed us printed itineraries for the day. Different groups were doing different things to spread out the access to the different areas and buildings around the historical district downtown. Our group's first activity was to walk a few blocks down and meet up with a tour guide for a walk through the capitol building. Then we were to go on a walking tour of the governor's mansion before settling in for lunch in a park area where the buses with the kids' box lunches for the day would be waiting for them.

"Blue Group," I called out to gather our kids to join us near the front of the bus. I waved the blue paper on which the itinerary had been printed over my head to draw the kids' attention. "Chip, count them off. We should have ten."

Chip looked at his identical paper and started calling off names, beginning with Sadie. When he'd checked off all the kids from the list, I waved the paper over my head and started walking down the street. By taking the lead, that meant Chip could bring up the rear and gather any stragglers.

I glanced down. Sadie walked right at my side and not with the small gaggle of kids chattering along behind me. She looked back at her classmates and let out a long sigh.

"You want to talk about it, kiddo?"

"No. It's my fault, so this is just my life now."

I bumped her a little with my hip as we walked. When she looked up at me, I smiled and said, "That's enough of that. We don't mope and wallow in self-pity in our family. You screwed up. Fine. Now you have to surf through some stuff. How you handle this will have a lot to do with how long your friends freeze you out."

"But Astrid is the one that's leading them. She was my friend and now she's not. She, of all of them, should understand what happened."

I nodded. "Maybe she's scared the same thing could happen to her, so she's overreacting."

Sadie thought for a second and then shrugged. "Maybe. But I thought she'd at least give me some sign that she understands."

I had the instant desire to make a catty remark about Astrid's mother. Instead, I said, "Give her some time. Soon, there'll be some other thing for all of them to focus on. Then it won't be all about you anymore."

"I hope so. I miss hanging out with them."

We'd reached the entrance to the Capitol building. I stopped and raised my blue paper over my head. I began counting heads and got to ten, followed by Chip at the back end of our group. He walked up and joined me.

A cheerful woman's voice from behind me said, "You must be my first group from East Elementary in Westminster. How is everyone on this fine October day?"

The woman wore an outfit from some period long ago with a long skirt and a white apron over top of it. She waved at all of us and said, "I'm Mrs. Tackleberry. I'll be leading your tour of the old Maryland State Capitol today. Before we get started, does anyone have a favorite fact you learned about Annapolis and the state government at school?"

A boy at the back raised his hand. "I know this wasn't the first capital. That was in another place for a while."

Mrs. Tackleberry nodded. "Very good. Yes, the state of Maryland was originally settled in the southern part of the state in St. Mary's County. The original capitol building is there along with some excellent exhibits about the early people and culture of our first settlers here. Does anyone else want to share?"

She waited for another student to volunteer a random fact for a few seconds then waved her hand in the air. "Very well. Follow me into the main rotunda where we will begin our tour."

We walked up some steps and entered the old brick and stone building. The halls were very grand with columns lining the walls and statues and artwork in between the columns and doors. Mrs. Tackleberry began her running commentary on the items and rooms we passed through. She gave a very entertaining lecture on the excitement of discussions in the state House of Delegates Chamber. I had to admit, I was learning quite a bit I hadn't been aware of before we came.

I became so engrossed in our tour guide's running commentary that I totally missed it when Sadie left my side and wandered away from the group. By the time I realized she wasn't there I had a moment of panic and I called out to Chip.

"Chip, where is she?"

He knew who I meant right away, and his head swiveled around, searching the broad hallway around us. Chip then looked straight down the hallway where we'd been moments before. "When did you last see her?"

"Back in the Delegates Chamber." I looked back down the hallway to the double doors leading into that room. "You take the group and stay with Mrs. Tackleberry. I'll go and look for her. Keep your eyes open in case she wandered ahead."

He nodded and I walked back to the room we'd just left. I heard Sadie's voice as soon as I got close to the entrance.

"You shouldn't be sad. I know we can help you find what you need."

A man's voice answered. "But it's been so long. How can you be sure you will be the one to do what I need?"

"Because I'm going to be the Queen someday."

I burst into the room, rushing to stop Sadie from saying anything else. She sat on a bench against the wall inside the door. A man in a period outfit similar to Mrs. Tackleberry's sat next to her. I relaxed a little seeing her with another tour guide. I was still angry at her for telling him her greatest secret, but maybe I could gloss it over as nothing more than a little girl's imagination.

"Sadie, there you are. What are you doing wandering off like that? You know better."

"Aunt Rose, this is Terrence. He's saying he's related to us and needs our help."

I took a second look at him using my other magical senses but didn't detect anything emanating from him. In fact, it was almost like he wasn't there at all. Something was very wrong here.

"Sadie, get up and come over here by me. Now."

She stood but didn't come any closer. "What's wrong, Aunt Rose?"

"You know better than to talk with strangers. Come over to me now." My hand twitched, wishing I had my sword. This was definitely an Unusual being of some sort and a very possible danger to my niece.

Sadie crossed her arms and her eyes flashed with power. "I'm trying to help him. He needs us, he's family, and I'm not going to come to you until you agree."

That was all the sass I was prepared to take from her. I walked over and reached out for her hand. As I did, I noticed the almost timeless air about the man. He wasn't from this time and place. I didn't know how Sadie had caused him to manifest, but we couldn't have a stranger from another time following us around. People would ask more questions. This definitely wouldn't help Sadie's image problem either.

I pulled her to my side and studied the man and said, "Terrence, I don't know why you're here, but you should know better than to scare children and involve them with your problems."

"But she's the first living thing to talk to me in hundreds of years. It must be because of our shared blood. The same is true for you now that she's helped me manifest forward in time."

"That's the second time you both have mentioned that we're related somehow. What do you mean?"

Terrence smiled. "I'm Terrence Goodfellow. I came here to Annapolis with a ship full of other Fae folk in 1754. I believe I'm your long-lost cousin. The same is true for young Sadie here. She approached me in my ghostly form when you all entered the chamber and told me I didn't need to be sad. She reached out and touched me and suddenly I became as you see me here."

"It's true, Aunt Rose. I could see him, but only a little bit. When I touched him, he became clearer. The power just came to me in a rush. I couldn't stop it, I swear."

This was all so much, so fast, and I had to come up with something to do quickly. Chip would be nearing the end of the tour soon and we were supposed to go on to the governor's mansion next.

"Terrence, I'm sure you're very nice, but Sadie is just a little girl. I'm sure you understand that there's nothing we can do to help you after all these years since your passing."

"Rose, you don't understand. I was cursed by the man who killed me. I was doomed to haunt these halls until freed by a powerful Fae magic. At the time, I feared it was an eternal sentence since there hadn't been anyone with that kind of power for centuries. I knew of a family rumor that one with such power would come someday, but I never put much stock in it. Now I know it was all true. Sadie has freed me from my eternal captivity and that means I can now go seek out my destiny in this place and time."

I breathed a sigh of relief. "Oh, thank the gods. You don't need us to do any of that. You are now free to go on your own. Go and make your way in this modern world. Just swear to me you'll never let on what you know about Sadie."

"Aunt Rose, we're not going to let him go from here without helping him. He's family. You can feel it if you'd open yourself up to the bond."

"It doesn't matter, sweetie. We're not taking him with us, and we can't stay here to help him. We have to leave in a few hours on the bus back home. Terrence will be fine on his own, won't you, Terrence?" I glared at the ghost trying to get my point through to him.

"Oh, yes, I suppose I can muddle through without your help. How bad could it be out there? I suppose I can at least invoke the Queen's blessing on my quest. That will open a few doors."

My eyes widened. "No, absolutely not. First off, she's not Queen yet. Second, people around here don't have kings and queens anymore."

"Oh, yes, that revolution you all had right after I died got rid of your ties to the old world." Terrence scowled. "But how will I find anyone to help me if I cannot invoke Queen Sadie's name for assistance? You must help me. Don't leave me alone again." He dropped to his knees with his hands clasped pleading his case to me.

I rolled my eyes. His melodramatic words weren't going to sway me. "I'm sorry for whatever happened to you, Terrence. But there's nothing we can do."

"But Aunt Rose—"

I shook my head and took Sadie's hand. "I said there's nothing we can do. Now we're leaving. Say goodbye to Terrence. He'll be fine on his own, I'm sure. He's a big ghost and way older and wiser than both of us."

Sadie raised a hand to wave. Terrence, still kneeling, waved back. "Goodbye, my Queen. I'll never forget you."

"Nor I you, Terrence."

I tugged at her hand, and we left the chamber. There was something about Terrence that didn't sit right with me. I mulled it over while we walked out in search of the rest of our group. If we hurried, no one would notice we were even gone. I hoped Chip managed to keep them moving and collected while I was gone.

8

Chip

Mrs. Tackleberry slowed to a halt at the far end of the central hall at the capitol. She smiled and said, "That concludes our tour of the capitol. Does anyone have any questions?"

When none of the children raised their hands, I stepped forward with a smile. "Thank you, Mrs. Tackleberry, for your informative trip through the building. What do you think, kids? Should we give her a big East Elementary thank you?"

The kids laughed and clapped for their tour guide. She smiled and said, "I'm so glad you enjoyed the trip through history here. Now, I believe you're due to head over to the governor's mansion for a tour there." She glanced around and then added. "I think you've misplaced one of your chaperones. That's interesting. If we lose anyone, it's usually one of the students."

"She's helping a student with something," I said. "She should be here shortly." I used my Guardian sense and zeroed in on Sadie's location. She seemed sad through our emotional link, and I looked around in her direction. I spotted her and Rose right away. They'd just exited the House of Delegates Chamber. I noticed a man in one of the tour guide outfits step out from the room and watch them walk away.

I ignored the stranger and said, "There they are. We're all here at last. Kids, let's form a line and get ready for our trip to the next stop on our tour." I took a minute to get them all squared away. That gave Rose and Sadie a chance to rejoin the group. My niece's frown said whatever had happened between her and Rose back there, she wasn't happy with the outcome.

My attention had to stay on wrangling the kids while we went outside. We had to cross several streets on our walk to the next destination and that required me to stay in the lead while Rose brought up the rear with Sadie. As soon as the next tour guide met us and took over talking to the kids, I drifted back to where Rose stood. Sadie's sadness had lessened a little bit. She'd joined the rest of the group and listened to the tour with the others.

"Rose, what happened back there? I saw that other tour guide you were with in the Delegates Chamber."

"That wasn't a tour guide, Chip." Rose checked around us to make sure no one else was close enough to hear. She leaned in close and said in a lowered voice, "That was the manifested shade of a former member of our family. He was a distant cousin who died several hundred years ago. Your niece thought it was a good idea to help him materialize here in this century."

"How did she do that?"

"I'm not entirely sure. It might have something to do with her ability to see through other Unusuals to their true selves. This time, she must have sensed the spirit lurking nearby and drew him out of the mid-world between ours and the next."

I checked to make sure the kids were still engaged with the tour and continued along behind with Rose. "What do we do? We can't have a ghost wandering around talking to people."

"We don't do anything. I'm sure once she leaves the area, he'll fade back into the mid-world. I'm pretty sure everything will be fixed once that happens."

"You're pretty sure?" I asked. "That's not the usual Aunt Rose, Fae princess confidence I expect from you. If there's a potential for a long-term problem, we should take care of it."

Rose shook her head and said, "I'm sure it'll be fine." She pointed ahead. "The kids are moving along the tour. We need to catch up."

I looked ahead and realized we'd dropped a little behind the group while talking. I picked up the pace and joined them in a large formal dining room, moving forward to stand beside Sadie who listened to the guide as he described the way meals were served here in years past.

The tour continued and then it was lunch time. I didn't have time to talk with Sadie or Rose much as we got the kids squared away with their lunches. The school had sent along box lunches for everyone, including Rose and me. I glanced in mine and pulled out an apple and took a bite. That was when I saw the strange man I'd seen with Rose and Sadie back in the Capitol building. He didn't look like I expected a ghost to appear up close. He wasn't transparent or glowing in any way. He looked mostly normal aside from the strange clothing he wore.

The other kids didn't pay attention to the strangely dressed adult in their midst. They'd seen others dressed like him earlier.

I hissed, "Rose."

When she looked my way, I nodded at the ghost lingering at the edge of the group. Her eyes widened, then she walked right over to him and got close so she could talk to him without any of the kids over-hearing.

I walked over to join them in mid-conversation.

"—You need to leave. Now," Rose said. "You need to go back to haunting the Capitol and whatever else it is you do."

"But I cannot. I thought about what you said. You are wrong, mistress. My queen has summoned me, and I must serve her. Surely you understand."

"I told you, she's not the queen yet, so there's no service needed. Go back to where you came from."

The ghost's expression left no doubt he was afraid of something. Rose wasn't picking up on it, though.

I jumped in. "I'm Chip Proctor. I'm Sadie's uncle. And you are?"

"Terrence."

"Nice to meet you, Terrence. Rose is right. You can't hang out around the kids like this. They'll start to ask questions."

"They seem nonplussed by my appearance here. I think they will soon adjust to my presence." He looked me up and down and added.

"You said you're her uncle? You're a human, a mundane. How is that possible?"

"Sadie's father was my brother."

Terrence gasped. "The Queen is a half-blood? How was such a thing allowed to happen? Have you no sense of propriety in this distant age?"

I shook my head. "Rose, this isn't going well. We need to resolve this. We're supposed to load up on the buses soon. We can't have him tagging along with us."

"We may not have a choice."

"What?" I asked. That was not the answer I was looking for. "Send him back."

"If he's bound to Sadie, he may have to remain close to her until he can be returned by magic. I hadn't considered that when I first encountered him, but it makes sense."

"How do we do that? There must be a spell or something we can do."

Rose nodded. "There is, but it's not something I can do. Fae are attuned to nature and life. Death is the purview of necromancers and other human magic users of great power."

"So, we're stuck with him?"

"I'm afraid so. Don't worry, Chip, I'll find a way to send him back as soon as possible when we return home."

"So, I may remain with my queen?"

I nodded. "Yes, but just for now. And don't refer to her that way. She's a little girl and not the queen yet. There's a lot of time to pass before that happens."

"But what should I call her?" Terrence's face carried a mixture of shock and bewilderment.

"Sadie. That's her name and it will do for now."

"It seems terribly disrespectful."

I said, "Things have changed. Many of the conventions of your time regarding rank and privilege have changed. You have to accept that and act in a way your queen would want in this time and place. Do you understand?"

"I do. I will endeavor to comport myself in a way that would do her honor."

I decided that was the best I was going to get from this guy. "All right, you walk with us, but at the rear of the group. When we get to the buses, wait for me to signal you before you get on the bus with us."

"Of course. What's a bus?"

I rolled my eyes.

Rose said, "Never mind. You'll figure it out soon enough." She scowled as she looked back at the center of town where the old Capitol was located.

I glanced back over my shoulder. There was a small patch of dark clouds forming over the Capitol's dome. It didn't look normal at all.

"Rose, what is that?"

She twisted around and stared back at the building behind us. "I don't know, but it's definitely magical in nature."

Terrence looked back where we were staring. Somehow, he managed to turn even paler in the face. "Oh, no. He's found me again."

"Who, exactly, has found you, Terrence?" Rose asked.

"The witch hunter. He tracked me here to the new world and was leaving a trail of dead Fae folk in his wake as he tried to locate me. When I died at the Capitol and he cursed me, I thought I was finished with him. Now he's somehow come back to find me through time."

"Uh, Rose, what's a witch hunter?"

"Let me deal with this." The grim look on her face didn't fill me with confidence.

"Are you sure?"

"You get the kids and Terrence here back to the buses. Load them up and get the driver to leave right away. Do whatever you have to do to get them away from here. I'll deal with the witch hunter."

Terrence's mouth dropped open. "How will you do this, mistress? You're not even armed."

"I'm not without the tools to deal with this. You two go, now. Get these kids out of here."

Rose started off at a jog back towards the Capitol.

"Uncle Chip, where is Aunt Rose going?" Sadie had come over. She waved at Terrence, then looked back at me.

"She has to take care of something important. We are going to get back on the bus to go home. Aunt Rose will catch up with us later."

"What about Terrence? Can he come with us now?"

"Yes," I said. "For the time being, Terrence will come with us. Now go throw away your lunch trash and get ready to line up."

I corralled the rest of the kids, getting them to clean up their lunches and deposit them in the park's trash cans. Then we all walked back to where the buses waited to take us back home. Terrence brought up the rear, walking behind Sadie. Every now and then, he twisted back to check on the growing cloud of dark magic above the center of town. I could tell by the look in his eyes, whatever manifested there filled him with terror. I hoped Rose would be okay facing it alone.

9

Rose

I kept up my hurried pace until I was back at the Capitol. I worked to slow my breathing while I slowed to a walk to go inside. I knew where I was heading. If this witch hunter had come back to life because of Terrence's return, then he'd show up where Terrence first manifested with Sadie. It was probably the power of what she did that drew him from whatever plane in hell he'd inhabited since his death.

Out of habit, my hand reached up to my shoulder to grasp my sword's hilt and I cursed. I was unarmed. I could really use my sword in the coming encounter. There was no way this hunter was going to back down peacefully. There would be a fight and I was going in unarmed. I guess I'd have to Jackie Chan things and use whatever I had at hand to deal with this guy.

I waved my hand, casting a glamour that distracted the tour guides and other visitors from noticing me. That would keep anyone from coming over and asking annoying questions. I'd drop a similar magic in place when I arrived at the Delegates Chamber. I didn't want to be interrupted once I was inside.

A loud shout from down the hall near the Delegates Chamber told me I was too late to avoid anyone finding out about the witch hunter. A man flew backward from the open doorway to slide across the marble floor. It was one of the tour guides and he didn't immediately rise when he stopped sliding.

I picked up speed and rounded the turn into the room just in time to see a blond-haired man dressed in an all-black pilgrim outfit. He fit the image right down to the silver buckles on his shoes, the breeches that reached to his knees and the long-waisted black coat buckled with a leather belt. A heavy silver cross hung on a chain around his neck. A tall black hat with a wide brim and a buckle on the hat band topped off the period ensemble.

He didn't see me at first. His attention was on Mrs. Tackleberry, who had backed up against the wall to my right.

"I asked you a question, Goodwife. Answer me or I will assume you an ally of the dark ones. Where is the Fae warlock named Terrence? He was here. I can taste his essence."

"I don't know anyone by that name. There's no Terrence who works here."

The witch hunter scowled and lowered his dark brown eyebrows. "Then you seal your fate as a follower of the dark one yourself." He raised his hand and started muttering as he pointed two fingers in Mrs. Tackleberry's direction.

I'd seen enough. "Hey, hunter man, why don't you tackle someone who knows what kind of scum you are." I let the power flare in my emerald eyes.

The hunter's eyes widened as he caught the flash of light behind my steely gaze. "I do not recognize your strange dress or understand why you adorn yourself in trousers like a man, but I know a Fae witch when I see one. Prepare to meet your fate."

His arm swung around my way and a wave of force drove forth from his fingers in my direction.

My magical senses felt it coming even though it was invisible to the human eye. I quickly swung my arms around in a broad circle to bring my forearms up in an x in front of me. I stepped back with one foot behind me just in time to brace against the attack.

I grunted as the power of his spell struck my rapidly erected barrier. I nearly buckled over backward from his strength, but I managed to keep myself upright. I held my arms crossed and ready for another attack and glanced at Mrs. Tackleberry. "Get out of here and close the door behind you."

She let out a squeal of terror and ran for the exit. The door slammed a second later.

"Now it's just you and me," I said. "Things are different in this age and place. My kind are no longer hunted for sport or persecution. Humans and the Unusuals live beside each other in peace now."

He let out a bellowing laugh. "Nothing like that would ever happen. No decent human would consort with the dark one's minions willingly. You have used your evil magic to put a spell in place to control the people of this place if what you say is even half true."

"I don't want to fight you, hunter, but know that I will end you if you persist in your quest to seek Terrence. End this and return to whence you came." I needed to try and send him back without a fight. He was too powerful to face without my sword, and maybe even a few friends for backup. I'd barely blocked his first attack and he didn't even look winded from the effort of it.

"I do not care what you want or don't want, witch." He reached inside his coat and drew forth a long, thin dagger. "I will end you with silver and cut out your tongue so everyone knows your crime as a spell caster for the dark one."

I shrugged. I'd tried to end this without a fight. Now I had to figure out a way to defeat him so he couldn't track Terrence and find Sadie in the process. I darted to the nearest table and picked up a heavy, round golden platter about eighteen inches across. I got to it in time to spin around and block his incoming blade.

A loud clang sounded as the two metal objects collided barely a foot away from me. I continued my spin, bringing up my leg in a roundhouse kick at his head.

He snarled in anger and leaped back from the follow-up attack.

My spin ended and I landed facing him. I brought up the golden plate with two hands, ready for the next attack.

"You think to defend yourself with dinner ware, witch? Maybe you are less powerful than you think you are."

"I'm plenty powerful. The plate's a distraction, idiot." I threw it at him like a frisbee and made a grasping motion with my hand. The

Maryland flag in the corner behind the speaker's seat tipped sideways. The pointed tip on the pole leveled at the hunter and flew right at his back.

He saw my gesture and twisted around, using the dagger at the last instant to bat aside the incoming spear. The flagpole kept going past him and embedded in the wood paneling beside me.

I heard voices over radios approaching from the hall outside. This wasn't going to end well if that was who I thought it was. I didn't need human police or security guards coming in to witness this fight. That was how people got killed and Unusuals got outed. I needed to keep this fight private.

I drove a two-fingered force lance of my own at the hunter with all the power I could muster.

He groaned and flew backward to slam into the far wall where the flag had stood seconds before.

Running to the door, I dove and gripped the knob in time to feel it start to twist from the other side. I sent a jolt of electricity through the metal and heard a man yelp on the other side. I followed the miniature lightning spell with a simple locking cant that should keep the door shut against most mundane attempts to open it.

"What is it you fear, witch?" The hunter had stood and stared at me by the chamber's entrance. He wiped at his mouth with the back of his hand and looked at the smear of blood there with a wry grin. "Perhaps the people here aren't so friendly to your kind as you say. Let them in and we'll see who they choose to apprehend."

The witch hunter waved a hand in the direction of the doorway, and I realized my error. The legends said these old-school hunters possessed strong power to dispel all sorts of magical energy and spells. The pounding on the door outside stopped as the door unlocked and swung open. Four State Troopers ran in, leaving Mrs. Tackleberry standing in the doorway behind them.

"Good gentlemen," the witch hunter said. "This woman is a witch and is guilty of consorting with dark and evil spirits. I charge you with her arrest so she may be tried and hanged like all of her kind."

The lead trooper pointed at the hunter. "Drop the knife, buddy. We don't have to end this with anyone getting hurt."

Another of the state police officers stepped around me to interpose himself between me and the witch hunter. I considered warning them he was dangerous with or without the dagger but decided to keep my mouth shut and see how this played out.

"I see she has placed you under her spell, or do you serve the dark one yourselves?"

The lead trooper shook his head. "We serve the governor and the people of the State of Maryland. Now I won't warn you again. Drop the knife or we'll have to tase you."

"I know not what that spell is, but I assure you, I'm protected against all manner of fell magics and spirits." He crouched to be ready for any attack and did not drop his dagger as instructed.

From behind me and to both sides I heard the other two troopers call out "Taser, Taser, Taser!"

There was a click and soft whine as twin barbs and thin wires shot out from both deployed tasers. For a moment, I worried the hunter's thick woolen coat would be too thick for the barbs. But I was wrong.

The witch hunter's body went rigid, and he stood there trembling for a second before he gasped and fell to the ground, the dagger clattering to the wooden floor beside him.

The two troopers closest to him ran forward. One rolled him over and the other kicked the dropped dagger across the floor out of reach. Then the first one knelt down and cuffed the hunter's hands behind his back.

"Check out his outfit, Bill," the lead trooper said. "Definitely old-school."

"Yeah," the other officer beside the downed suspect said. "He's a few weeks early for Halloween." He turned to me. "You all right, ma'am?"

"I am. I don't know why he attacked me and Mrs. Tackleberry that way. He seems to think we're witches or something."

"We get all kinds of crazies who come here to see the governor or the delegates when the legislature is in session. This isn't the first time I've encountered someone like him."

"Really?" I couldn't believe there'd been another witch hunter appearing randomly at the Capitol, but I wasn't sure. "Was there another one like him here?"

"Not exactly like him. This other one was more like one of those 'sovereign nation' wackos. He came to protest against the court making him pay taxes. That was last week's crazy. Honestly, ma'am, it takes all kinds."

The one named Bill, helped by one of the taser-wielding troopers, lifted the dazed hunter under his arms and half carried him from the room.

The lead trooper came over. His name tag said his last name was Crane. "I'm going to need to take a statement from you about the attack, if you don't mind."

"Are you sure that's necessary? I need to get back home."

Trooper Crane shook his head. "I'm afraid it is. We need all the information on what he did before we arrived. Now, tell me what happened before we were able to force the door open."

I made up a story about coming back to look for my cell phone, left behind on our trip. I told the trooper how Mrs. Tackleberry and I were attacked by the knife-wielding man in the Delegates Chamber.

Mrs. Tackleberry nodded, though she seemed a little scattered as she backed up my story. The trooper wrote down our account of the encounter and went over to talk to his companion who stood staring at the state flagpole embedded in the wall.

Beside me, Mrs. Tackleberry whispered, "I don't know what happened back there, but thank you for saving me. I can't explain what happened when you arrived, but I'll stick to your story on how it all went."

"Thank you. The less strangeness we have to explain, the better. Are you okay?"

"Just flustered. I've never had anything like this happen to me before. Most people who come here are happy to get the standard tour." She paused and then said, "Are you what he said you were? A-a-a witch?"

"Let's just say the less you know, the better. Stick to the story I told the trooper and we'll let the judge work it all out. That man was clearly out of his mind, right?"

She met my eyes and gave a half smile. "Right. I guess this'll give me a fine story to tell my husband when I get home tonight. He always tells me our lives are so boring. I think I'd like a little boring right now."

"You take care of yourself, Mrs. Tackleberry."

She walked across the room and pulled out her phone from her apron pocket. As she started to place a call, I walked over to the two troopers.

"Can I leave? I'd like to try and arrange a ride back to Westminster. The school buses left without me."

Trooper Crane said, "I have your contact information. I'll call you if I need any more information. You're free to go."

I nodded and left the chamber behind. I texted Warren as I walked out of the Capitol building. Hopefully, the investigator was available to drive to Annapolis to pick me up. While I waited for his answer, I spotted an old tavern sign on a side street nearby. I decided some food and drink were needed to replenish my mana and give me some time to think about what to do with Terrence. I was sure this wasn't the last we'd see of the witch hunter.

10

Chip

On the way back to the bus, I instructed Terrence to say as little as possible and sit quietly while we drove back to Westminster. The last thing I needed was to try and explain the stranger on the school bus. It was hard to get him to listen. The world of the twenty-first century awed him in too many ways to pay attention at first. He pointed at the cars whizzing by and I had to pull him out of the street at one point. I finally got him in line just in time to get to the bus.

The two other mothers on the bus introduced themselves to Terrence and I got on last of all.

"Ladies, this is Terrence. He's a family cousin of ours who is one of the Capitol tour guides. We invited him back to the house for dinner tonight."

Sally Green, a tall, slim redhead, asked, "Where's Rose? She's the official chaperone. We don't know who this guy is. He shouldn't be around the kids."

Terrence started to object but I shut him down with a glare. I said, "Sally, Rose had some important personal business to attend to and Terrence offered to come back with us. That's all. I take full responsibility." I tried shifting the subject of the conversation. "I'm curious.

How did your group do on the tours today? The kids with us had a great time."

Katie McAllen, Sally's chaperone partner, laughed. "Two of the boys thought it would be fun to play a prank and try to carve their initials on one of the antiques. Luckily, Sally caught them right before they started. She confiscated the old, rusty nail they were going to use and spent the rest of the time riding herd on them and their compatriots."

Sally rolled her eyes. "You neglected to add one of the boys was my own Kirk. That kid is going to be the death of me someday. He tries my patience every chance he gets."

"Surely a firm application of the strap would set the boy aright." Terrence's statement drew an immediate reaction.

We all turned with our mouths open to stare at him. He smiled, not realizing how his words landed in the modern world.

"Are you suggesting we beat our children, Mr. Terrence?" Sally asked. "I would never lay an angry hand on my boy."

Terrence opened his mouth to speak, but I jumped in before any more awkward words came out.

"Terrence is known as the family jokester. But I think this particular one missed the mark, buddy." I smiled and drew on my mana stores to press outward gently with my Guardian force against his chest while I held his gaze in mine. It kept him back in his seat and hopefully told him to keep his mouth shut. I kept the pressure up until he gave a quick nod.

"My mistake, milady. I meant no offense."

"Well, as long as you realize it's not something to joke about." Sally turned around to face the front of the bus as it drove up the ramp onto the highway home. She and Katie soon forgot it all and became engrossed in another conversation.

The moment passed and soon Terrence stared wide-eyed out the window of the speeding bus, marveling at the wonders of the modern world we passed on the way home. I realized this was probably the fastest he'd ever traveled in his life.

I leaned over his way and asked, my voice low, "It's a great way to travel, isn't it?"

"Am I to understand that all these other conveyances outside this wagon are for individuals to use to get around? I've never seen so many people or this type of construction in my life."

I checked the two ladies across the row. They weren't paying any attention and I went back to Terrence. "There's a lot that's new since you were last here. Don't worry. We'll take it slow until you get situated to how things are. You're family, after all."

"Aren't you afraid of what might have happened with the witch hunter? The princess could be in danger. No man of any worth would let her fight on her own."

"You'll find that Rose can handle herself in a fight better than any man I know. She'll be fine." As if on cue, my phone chirped. I pulled it out and glanced at the screen. "As a matter of fact, that's her now. She says she's meeting her friend Warren for a ride back home. I guess that means she handled the witch hunter just fine."

"How can you communicate with her with that piece of metal and glass? What magic is this?"

"It's not magic, Terrence. It's a very complex machine, sort of like a very fancy clock that does more than tell time. It can communicate over great distances. I'll show you more of how it works when we return home. For now, just keep track of your questions and we'll answer them when others aren't around to ask questions about who you really are."

"Perhaps that is best. We shouldn't let on that I am Fae. Thank you, Chip Proctor. I will save my questions for later."

He went back to staring out the window at the passing vehicles and the buildings and homes that could be seen along the highway. I prepared myself for an interesting night explaining advanced technology to a Fae from the 1700s.

The rest of the trip passed quickly. Soon we were back at the school parking lot. It was just before school let out and we all had to sign out our kids before we could leave. I left Terrence standing beside our minivan with strict instructions to interact with no one beyond a quick greeting.

Sadie and I went into the school office where I signed both her and Addison out a few minutes early. The secretary called down to Addy's classroom and had him sent up to meet us outside of the main office. Once he arrived, we all left to head home. I wanted to hurry and get out of the lot before the buses started to leave.

Addy was very interested in Terrence the minute he met him. "Why do you wear funny clothes? Where are you from? Do you always use weird words when you talk?"

I smiled as I drove and listened to the kids meet their cousin from long ago.

Sadie helped Terrence answer some of the questions. "Addy, this is a distant cousin. He was here before we became a country. Isn't that awesome?"

"Did you know George Washington?"

"I do not know anyone by that name. I'm sorry," Terrence replied.

"He's the first president. He was very important."

"I fear the only important person of whom I am acquainted is Charles Carroll of Carrollton. He is one of the colony's leaders at the state legislature."

I perked up. That name I recognized. "We live in the county named after him. He signed the Declaration of Independence."

"Declaration of Independence from what?"

"Why, the king, Terrence," Sadie said. "Everyone knows that. King George was the worst and we told him to go soak his head."

Terrence gawked at Sadie. "You can't speak to a king that way. It's disrespectful. You could lose your head for doing that."

"That was the point of the declaration, Terrence," I said. "We here in the colonies decided we should rule ourselves and became a country of united states. Maryland was one of the thirteen original colonies. Now there are fifty states that span the entire continent."

"I find that a little disturbing. There were some who resented the will of the King over us, but I, for one, believed in loyalty to the crown."

That surprised me. "But weren't you more loyal to your own leaders among the Fae?"

"There hadn't been a Queen for several hundred years and most of our nobles looked after themselves, even those among our family. It was rumored that a Queen would be born again, perhaps from among one of our own, but many of us didn't believe it. The human govern-ments of Europe had stopped much of the routine persecution of our kind, so we allied ourselves with the human leaders as much as our own. I wanted to discover other ways of securing our power in this new world."

He looked back at Sadie. "Of course, my Queen, that was before I came into your presence. Now I understand all that went before. My mother often said our family was blessed by the gods of Fae. I think she must have been one of the few entrusted with the truth about our lineage."

Sadie laughed. "I'm not the queen yet, silly. I have to grow up first."

"Yes," I said. "And we keep that secret very close, Terrence. There are people and Unusuals out there who are searching for her and would do her harm if they discovered who she was. That was one reason Rose stayed behind to deal with the witch hunter. We couldn't afford to have him track you down and find her in the process."

"I understand. I hope she deals with that vile man once and for all. He tracked me and I swore he was about to run me through with his dagger. I remember feeling horrible pain and then I woke up as a shade in that building. It wasn't until many years had passed and I real-ized her Majesty could see me that I thought I might have a chance at a life again."

"Call her Sadie," I corrected him. "You have to get in the habit of treating her like a normal human child from this time. People won't understand and it could cause problems beyond exposing her identity."

"I'm sorry, your Maj— I mean, Sadie. I am ever and always your dutiful servant."

Sadie giggled. "Thank you, Cousin Terrence. I hope you get to stay with us for a long time."

"I hope that is true."

I looked back in the rear-view mirror at Sadie, who looked up to meet my eyes. It was a "can we keep the puppy?" moment and I wondered what we'd gotten ourselves into when she brought the man back from the spirit world.

We got home quickly and pulled into the garage. Terrence was amazed when the door opened after I pushed the button on the remote. And turned to look back to watch it close after we pulled into the parking space inside.

Addy and Sadie piled out of the van and went inside the house via the door to the kitchen.

I called after them, "Get started on your homework. Sadie, you have that paragraph about your trip to write. Addy, get your stuff from today out and I'll be there to help you in a second."

Terrence had extricated himself from the seatbelt and climbed down out of the van. He looked around at the tools hanging in the garage. I figured most of the yard tools would look somewhat familiar to him. He pointed at the Tesla parked next to the van. "Is that another conveyance? It looks so sleek compared to many of the others I saw."

"Yes, it's called a sports car and it is very fast. I only drive it on the rare occasions when I'm out of the house on my own. Usually, I have the kids with me and need the van."

"What about your woman or servants? Surely, they can watch the children?"

"There's a lot you need to learn about these times, Terrence. First, I have no woman as you put it. Both Sadie and Addy's parents died, and I came down to become their Guardian. Rose helps me but doesn't live here. It's just me and the two kids."

"But the raising of children is not a suitable duty for a man. It's a woman's work."

I needed to nip this in the bud right away. I fixed him with a stern stare. "Not any more, Terrence. Do not cast aspersions on anything before you understand the circumstances. We can't hire regular help here because we have to appear to be a normal human family, and this is what humans like me do when we raise our kids without a wife or partner."

I hoped my little diatribe got him over that particular hump. He seemed chastised by the way his shoulders slumped when I was finished talking.

After a few seconds of silence he said, "I have much to learn, and I will endeavor to see what is the custom before I make any more statements about you and your role in the family."

I nodded, accepting his words of apology. He had to be a little freaked out by all that was happening around and to him. I needed to give him a little leeway.

"Maybe you'd like to come and help me work with Addy on his homework. He usually has some math problems to review. I'm sure arithmetic hasn't changed all that much since your times."

"I excelled at arithmetic. I would be happy to lend you aid in schooling the boy."

With that settled, I took Terrence inside and started acclimating him to his new surroundings. Our little home of three was now four, at least for the time being, and we all needed a little time to get used to each other.

11

Rose

After a half hour of near silence from me following picking me up in Annapolis, Warren said, "I don't know what happened back there, Rose, but you're usually more open about what kind of bad guy you're facing. Care to fill a guy in, since I'm sure you're going to ask for my help?"

I knew he deserved an answer after driving all that way to pick me up through mostly rush-hour traffic. The thing holding me back was Sadie. Warren knew about our family and her future, but this new display of her potential power wasn't something I wanted out there, even among my most trusted friends and family retainers. I decided in that moment, he, at least, was a safe person with whom I could share this.

"Something happened back there, Warren. Something bigger than I expected at this point from Sadie's growth into her power."

Warren chuckled. "I could've guessed it had to do with the kid. What did she do now, expose another shifter in front of a crowd of normal humans?"

"No, she brought forward a ghost from our family's past, manifested him in corporeal form, and accidentally ported a witch hunter forward along with him."

"I didn't think that was even possible. How far back are we talking here? I thought witch hunters were only around over a hundred years ago."

"More like two-hundred-fifty years ago."

"Wow!" Warren exclaimed. "That's quite a reach for a nine-year-old. How does she have that much power already?"

"That's something we have to deal with. If she's got this much power now, what's going to come along as she continues to grow up?"

"At least you dealt with the witch hunter. How did you dispose of the body, or did you just poof him away?"

"I can't poof a body away, Warren. My magic doesn't work like that. Also, I didn't deal with him in any final sense. He got tased by some State Troopers and they took him away in handcuffs."

"That's not good, Rose. Even without ID, they can't hold him forever. They'll have to let him out of jail eventually, and that's if he doesn't escape on his own."

"Exactly. That's what I've been going over in my head for the last half hour. How do I get into the Anne Arundel County jail, kill a prisoner, and get out again without getting caught?"

"Simple, Rose. You don't. That's a path you don't want to go down, even to protect Sadie. There has to be a better way."

I shifted in my seat and stared at him as he drove. "What do you suggest? I'm not letting him get away so he can track Sadie down and make an attempt on her life."

"I'm not suggesting that either. Let me make some calls. My guy at the Carroll County Sheriff's office should be able to find out how long they're holding this man. Once we know that, we can make plans to take him down when they eventually release him."

Warren's plan certainly sounded better in the near-term than anything I'd come up with. But I worried about anything that risked Sadie. Chip had made the decision to take Terrence home with them. That link back to the witch hunter would surely be enough to bring the danger too close to home.

"Do you think your guy at the Sheriff's office would be able to alert you before the witch hunter's release? If he could do that, then we could track him after he gets out and get him to a place where the ensuing fight won't be noticed by any bystanders or the authorities."

"Maybe. It's one thing to call and ask about the disposition of a prisoner once, especially a John Doe. Getting the deputies down there to tag him in the system for an alert about his release will be a big ask."

"This is important, Warren," I said. "You know what's riding on this."

"I know, I know. No promises, but I'll see what I can do."

I didn't like the uncertainty of that, but I also knew it was the best I could hope for. While I waited for Warren to follow up with his connections in law enforcement, I needed more information about Terrence and this witch hunter. I let out a long breath because I knew where I needed to go next.

"What's wrong?" Warren asked when I sighed.

"I'm going to have to tell Aunt Allura about this. She's not going to be happy."

"Why do you have to tell her? It's not like she'll see it in the news."

I shook my head. "It's not that. I need to ask her some questions about the family back then. She's old enough that she should have at least heard stories if one of her relatives was hunted down in the state capital by a witch hunter. Word of something like that must have made it into the family tales."

"From what you've told me in the past, she loves telling you about the old days, and the old ways."

"And the whole time, she'll use the past as an example of some-thing I'm doing wrong in this century. Still, I need to find out every-thing I can about this guy. That means I'll have to suck it up."

"Okay, but don't call me for a few hours after you leave."

"Why not?"

"Because she always puts you in a foul mood and you'll bite my head off just to get it out of your system. Go over and visit Chip. He's used to you harping on him about stuff."

I laughed. He wasn't wrong. "Fair enough. As long as you promise to tell me what you learn as soon as you hear from your deputy friend."

"Deal."

With that settled, the rest of our trip back to Westminster fell into random conversations to pass the time. He dropped me off at my car in the school parking lot a little after seven. As soon as I got in, I called my aunt.

Reston, the butler, picked up the landline phone after the third ring. "Yes, Miss Rose, what can I do for you?"

"I need to see my aunt tonight. It's important."

"The mistress is settled in her room for the evening. I believe she's watching Bridgerton and won't want to be disturbed."

I ground my teeth. I didn't have time to deal with my aunt's gate-keepers. Why didn't she get a cell phone like a normal person?

"Reston, this is urgent. It's about Sadie and it cannot wait."

"Very well, I'll inform your aunt you're on the way. Understand she will not be happy."

"She can pause the streaming shows, Reston. It's not the end of the world."

"Tell her that." He hung up before I could respond.

There was nothing I could do but go and get this over with. I needed to know what my aunt knew about Terrence and the witch hunter, if anything. It took me twenty minutes to navigate through town and get to the farm country on the other side. My aunt's horse farm lay in the lush rolling hills that made up this part of Maryland.

I pulled up in the large circular driveway out front and walked up the long stairs to the manor's front door. Reston pulled the door open before I could knock and gestured me inside.

"She's in her sitting room upstairs. If you don't mind, I'll let you find your own way. I have some tea steeping in the kitchen."

I wanted to call him a chicken for not coming along, but I let it drop. "I know my way."

I started up the stairs. Lili and I had played in this home many times after our parents passed. We'd often hide in the hidden space in the back of the linen closet outside Aunt Allura's sitting room. From there, we could hear her conversations with visitors she allowed in her upstairs sanctum. I smiled at the memory as I climbed the broad, formal staircase to the second floor. Lili and I had so much fun together growing up. We only had each other, after all.

I stopped outside the sitting room door to gather my thoughts. I didn't get the chance.

"I know you're lurking out there, Rose. Don't just stand there, come in. You're not a child playing games in the linen closet anymore."

Had she known all these years and never scolded us? Caught off guard, I was still pondering the past when I opened the door and stepped into my aunt's personal domain. Her sitting room served as the entrance into her main sleeping chamber and bathroom. The whole suite was quite spacious.

Aunt Allura wore a satin dressing gown and sat on a cushioned divan against the far wall opposite a large flatscreen television. The image paused on the screen showed a pair of actresses in eighteenth-century garb.

"Don't just stand there gawking at the television, Rose. You had something important to tell me so get on with it."

I shook myself, cursing inside at being caught off guard this way. Aunt Allura always made sure I knew who the senior matriarch in the family was.

"May I sit? This will take a little time."

"If you must." She waved her hand at an upholstered chair next to the divan. "Should I ring Reston to bring you some tea? Mine is still hot but there's not enough left in the pot for you."

"No, I'm fine." I paused to think of the best way to approach this. "A situation has presented itself with Sadie, Aunt Allura. I need to find out about our family's past in order to deal with it."

"What happened?" The mention of Sadie got her attention immediately.

I told her about Terrence and how Sadie had somehow brought him forward through time. "It wasn't just raising a ghost. He's really here and not as an old, moldy zombie, either."

"Really, that is quite a powerful bit of magic she used. However, that is to be expected from someone destined to be the future Queen of the Fae. Really, Rose, you need to do a better job of preparing her for the advent of power like this. She shouldn't be stumbling around fiddling with time travel spells and cavorting with spirits from the past."

I wanted to defend myself, but I hadn't gotten to the most important part yet. "That's not all, Aunt Allura."

"There's more. Don't tell me you let her keep the cousin from the past like a pet. She needs to send him back."

"Yes, I agree. He is still here, but for a short time only, I assure you."

"What else is there, then? Out with it, girl."

I swallowed hard, feeling like I was nine again and getting chastised for stealing a piece of cake from the kitchen. I hated it when she made me feel this way. "The gateway Sadie must've opened to bring our relative through stayed open long enough to allow another to follow him to our time."

"That is not good. Who is it that followed this long-lost cousin?"

"A witch hunter."

Aunt Allure straightened at the mention of the hunter. "Did you kill him?"

"No, he lives. He's detained by the human authorities for the time being, but he'll be released eventually. I came to you because I need to understand why this distant cousin of ours is so important to a witch hunter that they'd risk entering a portal to an unknown place to chase after him."

"What did you say his name was?" Allura asked.

"Terrence is his name."

"I don't recall my mother or grandmother mentioning anyone by that name in particular, though there was mention of a relative who dabbled with dark, forbidden magic and drew attention from human forces arrayed against such practices. Most of the witch-hunting efforts ended up rounding up innocent human women who had done nothing more than engage in herbalism and natural healing. In the case of our relative, though, my grandmother seemed to think he'd gotten what he deserved."

A pit formed in my stomach. What had Sadie done? "You think this Terrence is the same person as this dark wizard? That's not good."

"Why, surely you've got him hidden away somewhere safe away from the children. Just go and make sure he doesn't get out and wreak havoc on the modern world. Then get Sadie to send him back."

"He's staying with Sadie and Addison at the house."

"What?" Aunt Allura rose to her slippered feet. "Rose, you must go to the house and get him out of there right away. If this is the same dark Fae magician my grandmother described, he will surely try to use her powers for his own purposes."

I got to my feet, gave a half bow out of habit, and ran from the room. I raced to my car, leaving the mansion's front door ajar in my haste. I needed to get to Chip's before anything happened. I hoped I wasn't already too late.

12

Chip

When I came downstairs from settling the kids in bed, Terrence stood in the hallway by the steps staring up at the decorative lintel over the door to the study. I walked over to join him.

I said, "I always wondered why this doorway had that ornate molding on top when none of the others in the house had it."

Terrence smiled and seemed to have a faraway look in his eyes. "Yes, it's a curious collection of old runes for a home to have."

"Do you know what they mean?" I figured he might know more since he was from several hundred years ago.

He shrugged. "No, I have not the faintest idea what they might be for. I suppose they held some important meaning for the parents of the children. It's too bad you cannot ask them."

"Yes, it is. Is there anything I can show you around the home before I go and clean up the kitchen from dinner?" I started back around the stairs to head toward the kitchen.

Terrence said, "I fail to understand why you as the master of this home seem so intent upon performing mundane duties like preparing and cleaning up meals. A proper household has a staff to do such things."

"I told you, Terrence. It's a different time and I prefer to do it myself."

"So," Terrence said as he looked around the living room, "you are expecting no one else to come into the house this evening?"

I didn't understand the purpose of the strange question. "No, it'll be just us. I'll get you set up in the guest room here on the first floor after I clean up the dishes."

A glow flashed in Terrence's eyes and he grinned at me, though there was no humor in his eyes. "I won't need a room for the night. Neither will you." His hand raised and a bolt of dark energy flashed from his palm straight at me.

I didn't have a chance to draw on my mana to block it and the powerful blast connected with my chest, sending shooting pains out through my entire body. The magical blast stiffened every muscle in my body, and I froze completely still from the energy coursing through me. I tried to scream, hoping I might warn the children something was wrong. Bernard and Brunna would certainly hear it and could protect the children. Unfortunately, nothing came out when I tried.

Terrence walked over to my rigid body. "You are stronger than I thought. That should have killed you. Nevertheless, it will serve to keep you out of my way while I do what I must to seize my destiny in this time and place. With a child of such unexpected power under my control, I'll rule this land and all within it. Goodbye, Chip Proctor." He reached up and tapped my forehead with his extended forefinger.

I toppled over backward, unable in my rigid state to stop my fall or break free to attack Terrence. On the way to the floor, my head struck the corner of the hutch by the kitchen door. In a flash of pain and darkness, I lost consciousness and the room faded to black.

I fought against the darkness for a long time. Then I heard a distant voice. Though I couldn't make out the words clearly, it seemed familiar. I focused on the direction from which it came and forced myself through the miasma of pain and darkness to draw closer to it.

After what seemed like hours, I heard the voice again. This time I recognized it.

"Chip," Rose called. Her voice carried the unusual tint of fear.

"For the gods' sake wake up. She's gone and I can't find her without you."

That snapped me closer to her in a heartbeat. I saw a glimmer of light and I pushed to reach it. My eyes fluttered open at last, and I stared up into Rose's emerald eyes.

"Finally, you're back."

I struggled to sit up, but she put a hand on my chest and pushed me back down to the floor. "No, you've got a bad head wound. Lay still for a few seconds and get your bearings."

"What happened?" I struggled to make sense of why I was on the floor in the first place and what I had been doing in the darkness before.

"I don't know, Chip. I just got here. Everyone in the home is frozen stiff as a board just like you were until a few seconds ago, including Addy, Bernard, and Brunna. Where's Sadie? Reach out and find her, Chip. He must have taken her."

"Who?"

"Terrence. Don't you remember anything?" Rose gripped my shoulders with fingers like twin vises. "Snap out of the fog, Chip. Sadie needs you. He's taken her somewhere and we need to get her back."

I fought to remember what happened and it all flooded back into my mind. I saw the burst of black energy and heard Terrence's final words to me before I blacked out. "Terrence hit me with some sort of magic. He said it was supposed to kill me."

"Thank your Guardian powers it didn't, Chip. Now think. Can you sense Sadie anywhere? He can't have gotten far with her on foot."

My mind reached out, following the now ever-present link to Sadie and— found nothing. I could sort of sense her awareness somewhere, but I couldn't sense a direction or distance like I usually could.

"She's there, Rose, but it's clouded by something obscuring her from my senses. I don't know where she is." This time I pushed myself and sat up despite Rose's warnings to lay still. I twisted my head around searching the room. When I turned my neck, pain lanced through my head, and I reached up to find a matted, bloody mass of hair on the back of my head. I pulled my now blood-smeared hand away, absently touching my thumb to my sticky fingers as I tried to make sense of everything.

"Try harder, Chip. The longer he has her, the harder it'll be to get her back. He's a bad one, Chip. Aunt Allura told me who he might be, and she was right."

"You said the others are frozen?" I asked.

"Yes, Addy, Bernard, and Brunna are all upstairs and rigid just like you were when I got here."

"I need to check on them." I pushed up to my feet, reaching out to steady myself against the wall when a wave of dizziness and nausea swept over me. Everything I looked at had a hazy double image to it. My hand went to my forehead. "I think I have a concussion."

"Come sit in a chair." Rose took my arm and supported me as I stumbled over to one of the dining room chairs. "They're all breathing, so they're okay for now. You focus on where Sadie is. They'll come around like you did in time."

"What if they don't?" I couldn't find Sadie and my mind and worry went to Addy upstairs and under a painful spell I couldn't lift.

"Look, if it'll make you feel better, I'll call Hitch to come over and check on them. He might be able to break the spell."

"Do that. I'll try and clear my mind while you make the call."

Rose pulled out her phone and dialed the human wizard. She had a brief conversation while she walked across the room. When she came back, she slid her phone in her back jeans pocket.

"That's done. Now focus, Chip. Where's Sadie? You have to be able to tell me."

I closed my eyes and reached out with that part of my awareness born when the Guardian magic passed to me. Sadie was there, but far away, almost so distant that I was afraid I'd lose contact with her entirely. I twisted my head while I searched for her, trying to localize the limited sensation of connection. No matter what I did, though, I couldn't figure out which way Terrence had gone.

"She's there, Rose, but it's like she's a long way off. What time is it? How long was I out?"

"I got here close to nine o'clock. I found you on the floor then. It's nearly ten now. It took me an hour to check the house and then wake you up."

"I put the kids down at eight. He's only been gone with her for a few hours. He doesn't drive, so how far could he have gotten with a child in tow?" My worry welled up inside me and I channeled it into anger and a driving need to find my niece.

"Figure a few miles an hour. That could be up to four or five miles away by this point."

I panicked. "We should call the police. It shouldn't be hard to find a man dressed like he's from 1750 walking the streets at night with a nine-year-old girl in his arms."

"We can't do that, Chip. First, I found a pile of his clothes upstairs. My guess is you'll find some of your clothes missing from your closet. Second, calling the sheriff or the state police could alert others who search for the identity of the future Queen. Anything strange put out on an all-points bulletin over police radios like that is likely to bring other searchers close to us and Sadie. We don't need that with Terrence out there and us nowhere near enough to protect her."

"What other choice do we have, Rose? We have to find her." Desperation filled me and I stood up, wobbled and almost fell over before I sat back down.

Rose put her hands on her hips. "You're in no condition to search for her like this. I called Warren, too, and he's on his way. He might be able to sense the trail by smell or something. I'll ask Hitch to try and find her, too. I don't expect it to work. If Terrence has found a way to mask Sadie from you, Hitch won't find her. The Guardian magic is stronger than anything Hitch can do."

"You're not filling me with confidence here, Rose. What do we do?"

"I was counting on you being able to locate her. With that avenue cut off, I'm not sure what else we can do. We'll have to fall back on some old-fashioned detective work. Warren will be able to help with that."

A knock at the front door interrupted us.

Rose said, "Come in, Warren. It's open."

The werewolf private detective entered the house and sniffed the air. "I smell blood." He looked at me. "Is it all yours?"

"Yes, unfortunately," Rose replied. "What have you found out?"

"There's a radio report of someone carjacking a woman in a parking lot about three miles from here. He had a young girl with him. He pushed the girl into the car and held a knife on the woman, forcing her to drive away."

"That has to be them," I said. "I know it."

"It also means they're more than walking distance away now," Rose said. "We have to come at this differently if he's managed to take a car. He could be halfway to Baltimore by now."

"My guy at the Sheriff's office said they don't know who the woman is or have any firm ID on the car yet. Just that it was blue."

"That's no help," I said. "They don't even have a license number to search for."

Rose paced behind the chair where I sat. "It's more than we had a few minutes ago. Terrence needs Sadie for something. He'll keep her safe for now. Her power's no good to him if she's dead or injured."

"But for how long? We need a way to find her or find Terrence to get to her," I said. An idea popped into my frantically searching brain. "The witch hunter! He found Terrence once, long ago. He could find him again."

"That's a bad idea, Chip. We don't want that kind of evil on our side. Even if he helped us, he'd just go after Sadie once we found Terrence."

Warren added, "Besides, he's locked up in Anne Arundel County's jail. He's not getting out anytime soon. He's got no ID and they're not going to release him as a John Doe. Even if they were inclined to let him go, he doesn't have the means to bail himself out."

"But I do. Rose, the witch hunter is our only option. You know it."

"I don't like this, Chip."

"Give me another choice and I'll take it."

We stared at each other for a few seconds, then she looked away.

"Fine. We can try to enlist the witch hunter. But his kind are not to be trusted. They hunted our people to death back in the old times. He won't agree to work with us just because we ask. We need to come up with something he wants more than his desire to see all Fae and other Unusuals hunted down and killed."

I smiled. "I'm Chip Proctor. I haven't met a person I couldn't strike a deal with. Set up a meeting and I'll handle the rest."

Rose and Warren exchanged glances. The werewolf shrugged and Rose sighed.

"I can't believe I'm going along with this, Chip, but you win. We'll get the witch hunter out of jail."

13

Rose

I tugged at the bottom of the tight blazer. I hated dressing up. "This isn't going to work."

"Sure it will," Chip said from the driver's seat of his Tesla. "Warren confirmed he hasn't been released yet and no one has posted the bail set at his arraignment."

"But I'm not an attorney. No one is going to think I am simply because I'm wearing this monkey suit." This pinstripe pants suit definitely wasn't high on my list of warrior princess wear.

"You are the only one who can disguise yourself and has the skills to get him free. If you can't arrange bail, then you'll have to break him free. Either way, it's got to be you."

I didn't respond. We'd been over this already several times during the long drive to Anne Arundel County. Chip was right and this was the best plan we could come up with. I looked inside my shoulder bag, doubling as a purse in this instance. The bundles of cash Chip had provided were inside.

"Fine, but you owe me." I popped open the door and climbed out. My high heels clacked on the pavement as I walked. I tried to take my time so I didn't wobble as I walked. I hated heels like this. They weren't practical in a fight, and I couldn't remember the last time I'd worn any like them. Probably Lili's wedding to Bobby.

The bored sergeant looked up when I entered the double front doors to the jail's intake area. I concentrated on the simple magical glamor I'd put on to disguise my appearance for the deputies and cameras in case I did have to break out the prisoner.

I walked up to a bullet-proof glass barrier between me and the sergeant at the counter. She leaned forward to speak into an adjustable microphone jutting out from the countertop in front of her. "State your business."

"I'm an attorney appointed to represent a John Doe you have in your custody. I've come to post bail."

"Do you have a docket number for his case?"

I dug around in my shoulder bag until I came up with a slip of paper with a series of numbers and letters on it. "Here it is." I slid the paper under the gap in the barrier and waited while the sergeant read through the document I'd given her.

"It all seems in order. You have the cash or bond for the bail amount?"

I nodded and patted my bag. "It's all in here."

She pointed to a large steel door to my right. "When I open the door, go down the hallway to the metal detector. Once you're scanned in, they'll direct you to the clerk's office where you can pay the bail amount and sign out the inmate. Have a good day, counselor." She slid a new slip of paper with the bail information and docket number on it back through the slot in the window.

I grabbed the paper for the witch hunter's release and the sergeant reached under the counter. A buzzer sounded as she unlatched the door. I hurried over to pull it open before the buzzing stopped. A long hallway stretched ahead ending at a pair of armed guards and a metal detector. I handed over my bag to be scanned and walked through without a problem. We'd been prepared for this, so I'd left my usual backup dagger in the car.

They pulled my bag from the scanning belt and handed it back to me. The one officer's eyes lingered a little too long on my bust and I snapped my fingers. "Eyes up here, buddy. I'd hate to have to slap a harassment suit on the county because you can't keep your eyes to yourself."

"Of course, ma'am. The clerk's office is that way." He smirked as he said it and I walked in the direction he indicated. As I walked away, my sensitive Fae hearing overheard him say to his partner, "Damned lawyers. If I had her alone in a bar, I'd show her…"

I spun around. "Show her what, exactly, officer?"

"N-n-nothing, ma'am. Sorry for the comment."

It was my turn to smirk at his shock that I'd picked up his inappropriate comment. I turned back around and spotted the sign on the wall nearby marking the account clerk's office. I entered and walked up to a tall counter inside.

A woman came over as soon as I walked in. "Hello, are you here to bail out an inmate?"

"Yes, if this is the right place."

"It is. I don't recognize you from the usual lawyers around here. Are you new?"

"Um, no. I'm from Carroll County. I don't get down here to Anne Arundel County that often."

The woman smiled. "That explains it." She took the slip I handed her and walked over to a computer monitor on the counter. She tapped away for a few seconds and said, "Ten thousand dollars, does that sound right?"

"It does. I have it here. Is cash all right?"

"We usually only get cash from the drug dealers, but yes. That'll do." She pulled out a receipt book and then set a plastic device on the counter. It was about the size of a lunch box. It took me a moment to realize it was a paper money counter.

I dug in my bag and pulled out the pre-bundled bills Chip had gotten from his bank. The woman took them from me, being careful to keep them in view on the counter. She slipped the paper wrapper off each bundle and set the stacks of bills in the slot in the counter. The machine counted through each bill and the total number displayed on the LED screen.

"It all looks correct to me. Let me write you a receipt for the cash and sign off on your bail slip here." She scribbled the total on a duplicate receipt pad. She kept one copy and handed me the original. Then she signed the slip of paper I brought in with me. "You take that back to the sergeant at the front entrance. Your client will be brought out to you there."

"Thank you for the help."

She waved a hand to dismiss my thanks. "It's my job. Glad to help. I hope you get down this way again soon. It's nice to see a new face from time to time." She grabbed the two bundles of cash and walked back to a large safe in the corner. The thing looked like it dated back at least a hundred years.

I nodded and took my slip with me as I left. The two guards at the security checkpoint kept their mouths shut this time when I passed through the exit. I ignored them and walked back out front.

The sergeant waited for me to slide the paper back through the slot and read it carefully before leaning forward to speak into the micro-phone. "You can wait over there on that bench. It'll take them a while to process the prisoner for release."

I didn't like the sound of that but didn't really have a choice in the matter. At least everything seemed to be going smoothly so far. I sat down on the bench by the far wall and pulled out my phone to text Chip. He'd want to know what was going on.

It took almost thirty minutes before the steel door buzzed and a deputy came out. He gestured my way and waited while the witch hunter walked into the lobby. He wore his attire from the first time I saw him, minus the silver dagger. That was locked up in an evidence locker somewhere. The deputy returned to the hallway, pulling the door closed behind him, leaving the two of us alone in the empty lobby.

The witch hunter looked around and spotted me. He recognized me immediately despite my spell of disguise. "You! You dare to come taunt me here. If they'd returned my blade, I'd deal with you promptly and properly."

"I'd keep your mouth shut, unless you'd like to go back to your cell." I nodded at the sergeant behind the large window. She watched the byplay between the two of us with interest. She'd obviously heard the threat made against me.

The witch hunter wasn't an idiot at least. He picked up on the situation right away and moved slowly in my direction. Keeping his voice low, he said, "What kind of trickery is this, witch?"

"The kind that gets you out of jail and maybe finds a way to send you home to where you came from. If that appeals to you, then come with me. If not, I'll tell them to put you back in a cell."

He twisted back to look at the locked steel door and then back at me. "Do you swear not to hex me or otherwise mark my immortal soul?"

"I wouldn't even know where to start doing something like that."

"Swear it upon your family's honor."

He obviously knew something of Fae culture. I nodded. "I will not use magic against you or otherwise endanger your immortal soul. This I swear upon the sacred honor of my ancestors and forebearers."

His eyes still stared at me with suspicion, as if he were trying to see what trick I was playing on him.

I didn't have time for this. He was our only chance of finding Sadie and I needed him on our side. I jerked my head to the door. "Let's get out of here. I'll explain everything to you once we're safely away from here."

"Very well. Lead on, witch."

I stopped. "It's Rose. Call me by my name or go back to your cell."

"That is for the best, I suppose. I am called Gareth. Lead on, Rose."

With that settled, I walked out through the front door and turned right to where Chip was parked. He stood outside the Tesla, leaning up against the side.

"This is our guy?" Chip asked.

"Chip, this is Gareth, the witch hunter. Gareth, this is Charles Henderson Proctor, also known as Chip."

"Well met, Charles, though I know not why you stand in the company of a Fae witch."

Chip smiled. "Oh, she's not that bad once you get to know her. Are you hungry? I figure we could use a bite to eat, and it might be best to get things sorted out somewhere we can talk in private. I want to get my kidnapped niece, Sadie, back and you're the one she says can do it.

I know of a restaurant on the way back that has a private room in the back. How does Italian sound?"

I nodded. It was fine with me.

Gareth shook his head. "I do not know. I speak no Italian."

I rolled my eyes. This guy was way too literal for me, and Chip was going to have a field day with him if he didn't loosen up some.

"No, I meant Italian food," Chip said. He waved a hand in dismissal. "Never mind. You'll like it. Climb in and I'll call ahead so Tony knows we're coming."

"I'll get in the back," I volunteered. I wasn't letting this witch hunter get behind me where I couldn't watch his every move. He still saw me as his mortal enemy, and I didn't trust him at all.

"Suit yourself," Chip said. "I'm driving, so it doesn't matter to me."

I flipped the seat forward and climbed into the rear of the two-door sports car. It was a cramped fit, but I managed. It was better than getting a tire iron thrust through my back. Gareth got into the passenger seat in front of me. Once he was in, Chip closed the driver's door. It took us a little time to explain the seat belt to Gareth, but once that was sorted out, we got on the road.

14

Chip

I tried to keep up a good front of confidence while I drove to my friend Tony's restaurant in Reisterstown. My guts roiled in knots with worry about Sadie. I could pick up a hint of her presence, though like before it was without my usual sense of her direction. I pressed to try and reconnect to her with my nebulous Guardian power. As with my other attempts since her kidnapping, it met a solid wall of power pushing back at me and left me with a throbbing headache once again.

"Charles, you mentioned a Sadie that is missing. I can only assume her disappearance is connected somehow to my release from the jail."

"You're correct," Rose said from the back seat. "She's our niece and she's been taken by Terrence, the Fae man you were after when you arrived here."

"Your niece? The two of you are human and Fae. How is it you have the same niece?"

"My brother married her sister," I explained. "It's not all that hard to figure."

"Blasphemy!" The disgust dripped from Gareth's tone. "Humans and Fae cannot consort together. It's not natural."

I shot him a stern stare before returning my gaze to the road.

"Look, pal, I know a lot of things are different here from your world back in the olden times. At the end of the day, all you need to know is there's a little girl out there who's been taken captive by someone. Are you the kind of man who would stand by without offering your aid?"

Gareth was silent for a long time before answering. "When you state it in those words, I see perhaps I have been hasty in my judgement. I will help you, but I do not trust the Fae, even half-human ones."

I bit back an angry retort. His hesitation angered me. "All you need to remember is she's a nine-year-old girl. Once we get her back, we'll figure out how to send you home to a place and time where things make more sense for you."

Gareth fell silent and stared out his window as I continued to drive. I didn't press the issue, even though I wanted to. That wasn't the way to make a deal with a hostile opponent. You had to let them reach a point so they saw things from your direction and think they came to the conclusion you desired on their own. I'd let him stew in his own thoughts. We'd hash it all out at Tony's.

It was near noon when we pulled into the strip mall off Reisterstown Road. I parked in a row close to Tony's place. I'd texted him before we left about his back room, and he said it was available. I got out of the car and waited while Gareth and Rose extricated themselves from the passenger side of the car. Gareth stood back and watched Rose's every move as if he expected her to attack him at any moment.

"Come on inside," I said, leading the way into the restaurant nearby.

They followed me inside.

Tony's Italian Bistro had become a favorite of mine. He had been a friend and fellow football player when I was in high school. We'd reconnected since I'd been back taking care of the kids. I made the drive over to his place a few times a year for dinner, usually with the kids in tow, though I'd brought Patty here once on a date. This was the first time I'd come at lunchtime.

"Chipster!" Tony greeted me as I walked in with Gareth and then Rose behind me. "I thought you'd forgotten about me. It's been a while." The former offensive lineman was bulky in high school. Now, nearly twenty years later, he was best described as rotund.

"I'd never forget about you, Tony. How could I?"

"I have the back room ready to go as you requested. Is this some big business deal you're putting together to get back into the Wall Street game?"

"Yeah, something like that." I nodded and he led the way through the busy dining room to a door that led to a small rectangular room with a rectangular dining table and chairs inside.

"This'll be perfect. We need the privacy."

Tony dropped three menus on the end of the table closest to the entrance. "I'll take your order myself to make sure you aren't disturbed by anyone you don't know and trust."

"You've always had my back, Tony. Thanks." I waited until he left and then took a seat at the end of the table. Rose grabbed the seat on my left and Gareth sat down on my right across from her.

"And you know this guy how?" Rose asked.

"Tony watched my blind side on the O line and kept overzealous pass-rushers off my ass back when I was playing ball in high school. We've kept in touch, and I've brought the kids here a few times over the years."

"Can we trust him not to listen in to our conversation about this situation?"

"Yes, Rose. I'd trust him with my life and the lives of the two kids. He's a good guy. He'll be discreet and leave us alone to talk. Let's order our food and then we can have our privacy."

I had to help Gareth choose. I opted for the chicken piccata and pasta with red sauce. I was pretty sure he'd never had spaghetti before but there was always a first time and Tony's fare was excellent.

Once we were alone after giving our food orders, I leaned back and rubbed at my temples. My head still ached from my earlier attempt to locate Sadie.

Rose noticed right away. "Still no luck finding her?"

"No, the harder I push to break through, the more the barrier pushes back. It's infuriating."

Gareth's puzzled expression led him to ask, "You can sense your niece?"

"Not anymore and that bothers me. I can tell she is alive, but I cannot pinpoint her location like I usually can."

Gareth said, "Terrence is an accomplished warlock and not to be trifled with. He's caused the deaths of several well-trained hunters sent after him. I was called in from Boston because no one else could catch him."

"What was he doing that was so bad?" Rose asked. "My aunt had heard of him from her older relatives as a child but never what made him so evil that a witch hunter like you was sent after him."

"Like all your kind, he consorted with demons and other dark forces."

"I don't consort with demons," Rose said. "I kill them like any sensible person does when you encounter them." Rose continued. "This is a waste of time, Chip. This guy isn't going to overcome his prejudices and he won't help us in a way that will protect Sadie. We need to send him back to jail."

"We can't. And I won't just cut him loose to wander the twenty-first century and get into trouble here." I looked back and forth between the two of them. "I can't do this alone. I need you both. One of you is the only one who can locate Terrence and the other is the only one I trust to protect Sadie against everything we encounter. You two have to find some common ground. There has to be something that you both can agree upon."

I leaned back and waited for them to come up with an answer. It was a method of negotiation I'd used before, just never in a situation so dire.

For a long time, the pair stared at each other across the table.

Tony rapped at the door and broke the stalemate. "Can I come in with the food?"

"Come on in, Tony. We're starving."

The door opened and Tony came in holding a large tray filled with our lunches. He made sure everyone had their orders and asked, "Anyone need drink refills before I go?"

"Thanks, Tony. We're good," I said. "I'll come get you when we need you to come and show us the dessert tray."

"I've got fresh tiramisu and cannoli. You're going to love it."

I waited for Tony to go and started in on my plate. I stopped when I realized neither Rose nor Gareth had stopped staring the other down.

"Time out. You two eat. I don't want to hurt Tony's feelings. This food is excellent and maybe breaking bread together will get us over our preconceptions about each other."

Rose looked away first and picked up her fork. After a few seconds, Gareth did the same. I went back to eating my first bite and closed my eyes as I savored the delicious, perfectly cooked chicken parmesan. The tangy sauce had my taste buds singing as I chewed.

A surprised grunt of pleasure from beside me had me smiling. "It's pretty good, isn't it?"

"I was not sure I would enjoy the dish; however, this is perhaps the best chicken I've ever eaten." Gareth switched to his side of spaghetti. "This noodle— What did you call it?"

"The pasta," I answered. "Yes, it's cooked to perfection. Tony knows his stuff."

"I have to admit, Chip," Rose said, "this is amazing."

"Good, so we have found we can enjoy a meal together. That's a start. Now, there's a little girl out there who needs rescuing. Can we agree that needs our joint attention, too?"

I waited while the two finished the bites in their mouths. When they had, I continued. "We need to work together. We don't have to be friends, just colleagues in this endeavor. Once that's finished, we can go our own ways."

Gareth's brow furrowed in concern. "I don't know what I can do in this modern world. I do not fit in here."

Rose nodded. "If it is possible, I promise we'll find a way to send you back to your time if that is what you wish."

"That is what I wish. For now, I will lend what assistance I can to find Terrence and end his plans in this time and place. One thing I do not understand is what he wants with the girl. A Fae child in my experience has little in the way of power or ability that he would desire."

Before Rose could do more than shoot me a stern glance, I made a decision. "Gareth, my niece is special. She is already strong in her power. It was she that opened the portal that brought Terrence, and you, here to this time."

"How? Such a thing would take a person of great power and skill."

Rose said, "Just know that she is special, and her power is considerable, though unpredictable. Terrence knows about this and probably has a way to use her to augment his own abilities."

Gareth nodded. "It is the power he uses that I'm able to track. If he has access to even more strength, then I should be able to locate him wherever he is in this area."

"Good, because that was my next question," I said. "Where is he right now? I would like to get Sadie back this afternoon if possible. She's already been with him for almost a day now."

Gareth set his fork and knife down. He leaned back in his chair and closed his eyes. He muttered something under his breath, followed by an Amen. He crossed himself twice and then opened his eyes suddenly.

His eyes darted to the closed door. "He is close, perhaps within a hundred yards of us."

"What!" Rose exclaimed. She jumped up, knocking over her chair in the process.

The door to the small room opened at the same time and five bulky figures in dark overcoats and black clothing burst in on us. They were all men, each with tattooed faces. They carried wicked-looking, curved daggers.

Gareth kicked back from the table with one booted foot, barely avoiding the first of the assailants who came in with his blade swinging down at him.

The witch hunter leaped out of his chair and snatched up the steak knife from the table, slashing at the face of the man who'd attacked him. He scored a deep gash across the man's cheek, and he fell back shrieking.

"These are warlocks," Gareth called out. "They have great power. Be on your guard."

Rose executed a perfect spinning kick that connected with the jaw of the man attacking her.

His head snapped to the side with a crack, and he crumpled to the ground with a broken neck.

I barely had time to do more than throw up my hands and raise my Guardian barrier before the other three attackers piled on top of me. The force of their rush knocked me over backward. The last thing I remembered was the back of my head striking the edge of the long dining table. Then everything went black as I was knocked unconscious for the second time in two days.

15

Rose

Chip hit the table and went down with all three of the warlocks piled on top of him. I rushed to get to him, but Gareth got there first. He picked up the first of the warlocks and flung him to the side with a show of amazing strength.

The warlock collided with the one with the slashed and bleeding face. The pair collapsed in a heap by the door.

Gareth reached for another of the black-clad attackers as I reached Chip's side. I picked up Chip's plate of half-finished chicken parmesan and brought the heavy ceramic dish down on the head of the other warlock who'd knocked Chip to the floor.

He groaned and twisted around to look up at me. His eyes flashed with power, and he pushed at me with one hand. The spell he released completed the powerful blow and knocked me all the way back against the wall.

The air pushed out of my lungs when I struck the wood paneling. I struggled to regain my breath while I stumbled forward to face the warlock who now stood above an unconscious Chip.

The warlock's eyes flashed with silver again and I prepared for another spell to come at me. I was still struggling to breathe and was in no position to block the next spell. I pushed off with my right leg, diving to the side to avoid the incoming magic.

A jet of flame scorched the wall where I had stood a split-second before.

With a croaking gasp, I dragged much-needed air into my aching lungs and rolled to my feet. I drew upon my own power and pointed a forefinger at the warlock. Green lightning lanced out at him.

His eyes widened as the thin bolt of lightning split into tiny strings of power that outlined his whole body. The energy drew upon his own power before winking out with a flash of light. His mana drained by my spell, the warlock lifted his curved blade and readied himself to charge at me.

He only took one step before Gareth came up behind him and buried one of the curved daggers in his neck right above the collarbone. Blood fountained up around the metal.

The warlock wavered and his hand reached up to grab at the hilt of the dagger in his neck. Then he toppled twitching to the floor.

I stood up from my battle crouch and took in the rest of the room. All five of the warlocks were dead, four of them at Gareth's hand.

"Are you well, mistress? Your hair is smoking."

Gareth's voice startled me back and the heat of the singed hair and burns on my left side sank in. I pushed the pain away and ran forward. "How's Chip?"

"He's breathing, but I fear he took a strong blow to his head."

I knelt down beside Chip and checked him quickly from head to toe. There was no sign they had stabbed him with their daggers. He was lucky. The welt and bloody gash on the back of his head was right next to the one from the previous night. It would probably need stitches, but we'd deal with that later. We needed to go after Terrence. If he was this close and brought help, then there was a chance Sadie was nearby.

"Gareth, where's Terrence now?"

"I cannot tell you. I may only pray for guidance once a day."

I bit back my ire at his answer. Magic was finite, even divinely granted magic. "You said a hundred yards. He must be in the parking lot with Sadie."

I raced out the door, Gareth right behind me. I passed several of the servers who were tending to a wounded Tony lying on the floor outside our room. He must've tried to stop the intruders.

Outside the restaurant, I skidded to a stop on the strip mall sidewalk. They had to be in a truck or a van with all the people he brought to attack us. I scanned the nearby vehicles and stopped at a large, black delivery van parked across the lot from Tony's place. Terrence sat in the front passenger seat. Another black-clad figure sat behind the steering wheel. I didn't see Sadie.

Terrence leered at me, showing his teeth, and pointed towards the parking lot exit onto Reisterstown Road. The van started and drove off at high speed, weaving through the parked cars in the middle of the lot.

I sprinted down the sidewalk, heading to reach the exit before he did. I wasn't sure what I planned to do if I beat him there. That would be something to figure out if I was fast enough.

It was going to be close.

As I ran, I drew upon all the remaining mana deep inside me. If I could disable the vehicle somehow, we could catch them and get Sadie back. She had to be in the back of that van.

They reached the exit first. The driver ignored the red light at the parking lot's entrance and took the right turn wide to head north. I feared he'd roll the top-heavy vehicle, but the van remained upright.

I released the spell I had planned in a desperate attempt to reach them. Thick vines sprouted from the cracks in the pavement right behind the van, long spike-like thorns jutting from the wrist-thick twisting branches. It wasn't in time to stop the van, but it did halt all the rest of the traffic north and southbound on the road. The wall of vines grew until it reached a height and thickness of ten feet stretching across the road. No one would be following them in that direction until the county road crews came and cut back the sudden growth in the way.

My shoulders slumped and I turned to head back and check on Chip. I bumped into Gareth standing directly behind me. His thick shoulders and strong chest startled me, and I stepped back.

"Your magics almost worked. There is no failure here. We will find them and return your niece to you."

I walked back towards the restaurant. Gareth fell in beside me.

"How did they find us?" I asked aloud. "Did they follow us to the jail and then here?"

"I fear it is my fault."

I shot the witch hunter a look. "What do you mean?"

"Terrence and I are linked. That is how I can find him. He can use the same link to find me."

I didn't understand. "What do you mean by linked?"

"Terrence and I knew each other when we were younger. We courted the same girl once. I knew nothing of his Fae nature. One winter, we skated on an icy pond with others by the village commons. The ice broke beneath us, and we both were pulled under. The evil sprite who lived in the pond had to draw upon some of the power within each of us to revive us before floating us back to the surface where people struggled to recover our bodies. Something in that sprite's magic tied us together. The girl lost interest in both of us and eventually I moved to Massachusetts Bay Colony to begin my education there. When Terrence began committing evil acts all the way down in Maryland, our strange bond remained. I could sense the terror of his victims all the way in Massachusetts, even though I didn't understand from whence it came at first."

"Is that part of the reason you became a witch hunter in the first place?" It might explain his zeal in hunting down Terrence and how he was drawn to our time along with his nemesis.

"Yes, I tried to find the source of the pain I felt, eventually training myself to sense pain from all those bound by evil powers. Only later did I discover the true source of what I sensed. I prayed to the Almighty to grant me the power to locate the source of the evil and I was granted the ability to do so once each day."

I'd heard of such divine abilities granted by the powers of light on some humans. It was similar to the way Chip had gained his Guardian powers from the ancient Fae. I hadn't met anyone else who had anything like that until now, though.

Sirens sounded in the distance, and I started running back to the restaurant. "We need to get Chip out of there and all of us gone before the police seal off the parking lot. Hopefully, we can get away before anyone identifies us."

"But the staff at the tavern will surely be able to identify us?"

"Let me deal with that. You pick up Chip and take him out to the back of the car. I'll meet you out there."

I ran inside. Tony had sat up and was propped against the wall by the door. He looked up at me and shook his head. "I tried to stop them. I really did."

"That's okay." I knelt beside Tony while Gareth squeezed by to get Chip. "Tony, call the staff over here; I have something to tell them."

Tony took a breath and strained to look around while he called out, "Everyone, come over here. My friend has something to tell you."

When they all had gathered around me, he nodded.

I let the last dribble of mana inside me out as I looked around, emerald fire lighting up my eyes. All the humans stood transfixed by my gaze. I waited until Gareth passed back outside carrying Chip before I said, "The people eating in the back room ran out before you could see them. You cannot identify them or describe them to anyone." The power in my words, infused with Fae magics of disguise and secrecy, filled each of them, including Tony. Their eyes fogged over, and I stood. As long as I was gone before their eyes cleared, they'd remember nothing of me and my companions.

I ran out to the car. Gareth stood with Chip over one shoulder trying to open the locked Tesla door. I raced to his side and dug Chip's keys from his pocket. I unlocked the doors and helped get him into the rear. Then I jumped into the driver's seat and waited for Gareth to get in. We pulled out of the parking lot just in time. We passed a line of police cars heading back down the road towards the strip mall.

"What do we do about Charles?" Gareth asked.

"We'll drive back to Westminster and visit the emergency room. I can come up with a plausible story about Chip falling and striking his head. His Guardian magic will heal him fast enough, but he does need stitches. We'll get him patched up and then talk about how to deal with Terrence now that he has found assistance here in the modern world."

"Those warlocks are similar to ones who attended Terrence back in my time. It may be their coven continued on beyond Terrence's time to exist in the modern world."

"It's certainly possible," I said. "I didn't recognize them, though. They aren't from any recognized group I know." I thought for a bit while I drove. "I think I need to visit the Sisters of the Moon. They might know which group this is and where I can find them."

"They sound like witches," Gareth said. His tone dripped with contempt.

"They are. If you're to come with me, you'll handle them with respect and honor. They are good women who help many in the community, human and otherwise, with their magic."

"I do not consort with witches."

"I'm not asking you to marry them. But if you want to find Terrence faster than your daily prayer locator, then we need their help."

Gareth got quiet. I noticed he did that often when he ran up against his prejudices in the modern world. So far, he'd handled the changes well. I hoped that remained the case.

Chip groaned and woke up right before I pulled into the parking lot at Carroll General Hospital. "Dammit, Rose, I bled all over the upholstery."

"I save your ass and that's the way you respond? Next time, I'll leave you with your friend Tony to explain five dead cultists to the police."

"Oh, God, Tony. Is he okay?"

"Yeah, though I had to cast a spell that clouded their minds so they couldn't remember us being there. That way the police won't find us. You can check on Tony later. Right now, let's go get you stitched up by the ER docs. Then I'll fill you in on everything else that happened after you decided to sleep through the attack."

I smiled back at him when I said the last, trying to lighten the mood a little. We were lucky and had underestimated Terrence and his ability to find help in the modern world. If we were going to track him down, we had to start taking the fight to him.

16

Chip

I walked out of the main entrance of the hospital ER and searched for Rose. I wasn't sure if she was in her car or my Tesla. She'd left and taken Gareth home to get some modern clothes. The crisp night air caused my breath to show as I let out a long sigh. The docs and nurses had kept me as long as they could before I put my foot down. I had refused to stay overnight as a precaution for my head injury. I wasn't staying in a hospital bed while Sadie was out there a prisoner of some psycho cousin from the past. Besides, this whole thing was my fault. I was the one who told Rose we should take the guy home with us.

My phone buzzed. I glanced down at the text message from Rose.

Pulling up now.

I waited while she drove up to the circular entrance driveway in her Firebird. I got in the passenger seat. "Where's the Tesla?"

"Plugged in at home safe and sound." She pulled away and left the parking lot.

I twisted around and looked in the back. "Where's Gareth?"

"He's at the house guarding Addy with Warren."

That surprised me. "He's okay with a werewolf in the house?"

Rose chuckled. "It was a bit tense when Warren first showed up. I've convinced them both to stand down and be good for the sake of the children."

"At least Addy's okay. Sadie's out there all alone with that monster and his new minions. Any luck on tracking them down?"

"Warren didn't have any ideas based on our limited descriptions. Maybe if we'd had a photo of their face tats, he might have seen something like a gang symbol. Without that, he has no idea."

Despite the throbbing headache from my injury, I reached out to find Sadie. The effort needed was definitely affected by my pain and concussion. I pushed out in search of her anyway. Once again, I had a nebulous sense that she was there, somewhere, in the distance, but I couldn't localize it or determine a direction like I'd been able to do countless times before.

"What are you doing?" Rose asked. "You look constipated."

"I have to connect with her, Rose. I can feel her and know she's alive and unharmed, but that's it."

Rose let out a long breath. "We'll get her back, Chip. Gareth found Terrence once before. He will track him down again."

"We can't wait for him to take days to localize the position." I pounded my fist on my knee. "There has to be something else we can do."

Rose grimaced and paused a second before saying, "I was going to take you straight home before I ran down a lead. Tell me the truth. How are you feeling?"

"Like I got hit from behind by a baseball bat. But I'll be fine. I can already feel the whole Guardian thing healing me up. I'll be good as new in no time."

"Okay, I'll take you with me, but you follow my lead. She shouldn't cause us any trouble, but she doesn't like strangers."

"Who are we talking about here?"

"Jessica. She's the leader of the largest coven around, the Sisters of the Moon. If there's a gang of dark warlocks around the area, she'll know about them."

"Don't worry about me. I get along with everyone."

"She doesn't. That means no trying to drop one of your Chip

charm bombs and expect it to go the way you want. You can come with me, but keep your mouth shut. I'll deal with Jessica."

I wasn't in the mood to argue, and a wave of throbbing pain hit me at that moment, so I nodded and left it at that. With my eyes shut against the oncoming headlights as Rose drove, I was able to lessen the pain some, but it didn't go down by much. I leaned my head against the back of the seat and tried some deep breathing to work through the pain.

It felt like a few seconds later when Rose gripped my arm. "You coming?"

I must've fallen asleep and was out for more than a few seconds. I looked around to see where we were. Rose had parked in an old, run-down trailer park. She had pulled up the car in front of a single-wide model with peeling white paint and several boarded-up broken windows.

"This is the home of the leader of the local witch coven? She doesn't worry much about appearances, does she?"

"No talking, Chip. I'm serious. You piss her off and she'll make us leave without helping us. We need her, not the other way around."

I opened the door and climbed out without answering. Rose came around and joined me in front of the rickety wooden steps leading up to the bent-up screen door. It didn't close all the way and waved a little in the slight breeze. The inner door was closed.

"Come on." Rose mounted the steps, pulled open the screen door all the way, and reached up to rap on the wooden door. It popped open before her knuckles connected.

"Enter, Princess. Your male companion may come with you as long as he understands the protocols." The voice came from the darkness inside the trailer.

Rose motioned with her hand at her side for me to follow and she slipped inside. I followed her. A single candle in a glass mason jar flickered on a low coffee table in front of a large recliner. In the chair sat the largest woman I'd ever seen. She had to be every bit of five hundred pounds. She was definitely not what I was expecting. Her long dark hair may have been brown, brunette, or black. I couldn't tell in the dim light.

"Well met," Rose said, with a dip of her head in a slight bow. "Chip Proctor, meet Jessica the Fair, leader of the high council of the Sisters of the Moon."

Jessica's cheeks dimpled as she smiled my way. There was no mirth in her eyes, though. "So, this is the vaunted Guardian of the future Queen? He doesn't look like much, Princess. You must have your hands full with this one."

I bristled at her tone and jeering glance. "She knows about Sadie?"

"Of course I know. Nothing happens in this county that slips by my notice. Don't worry. I care nothing about the affairs of the Fae nobility, and I know the value of a secret kept. It has served me well over the years. Now be silent and let your betters carry on with our business."

I opened my mouth to protest, but Rose held up her hand. "Shut it, Chip, or go back to the car. It's your choice."

My mouth clapped shut and I ground my teeth in frustration and anger at the witch's tone. It wasn't like me to react this way, but my brain wasn't acting like itself right now and I needed to keep a tighter control over myself.

Rose waited to make sure I listened and followed the instructions before she continued. "Jessica, I have a question about a local gang of warlocks operating somewhere in the area. I haven't met them before. They attacked us earlier in broad daylight at a public venue. We had to kill five of them before we could escape. We were able to cover up the worst of it before the authorities arrived, but it was close."

"I dislike those who are careless with their identities in the Unusual community. Describe these warlocks to me. Perhaps I know of them."

Rose ran through what they looked like, spending a lot of time on their facial tattoos. When she finished, she said, "They attacked without warning or provocation and may be linked back to someone we seek."

Jessica reached out and picked up a large Yeti jug from a small side table. She sipped at the metal straw for a few seconds before setting it down. "This wouldn't have something to do with a massive flare of magical energy I sensed to the east a few days ago. It had the flavor of the Fae to it, but it died down before I could send anyone to investigate it."

"It does," Rose said. "Sadie is coming into her power and released a danger from the past who must be tracked down and dealt with."

Jessica nodded. "The men you describe sound a lot like a gang of wannabe warlocks who hang out over in Frederick County. They can't decide if they're a biker gang or serious practitioners of the magical arts. They have links to a long line of warlocks dating back several centuries."

"What is their name?" Rose asked.

"The last I heard, they went by the name Dark Travelers, but that may have changed. I don't know exactly where they hang out, but they have been spreading the word they are linked back to a dark and ancient magic of one sort or another."

"And you haven't dealt with them? I thought the Sisters of the Moon would be a little more proactive about such a group in their own back yard."

"Princess, if I had a dollar for every jumped-up excuse for a coven who thought they'd accessed ancient dark magics, I wouldn't be living in this dump. Besides, they haven't caused any trouble until now."

Rose nodded. "They found a leader who can connect them with the very power they seek. I just wish I knew how Terrence found them so quickly after getting here."

"Perhaps he searched for an artifact from his time and discovered it in the possession of the Dark Travelers. I hope you deal with them promptly. They need someone to dispose of them."

"I was hoping you might lend us some aid," Rose said. "This is technically a coven matter."

"They didn't attack in this county. You were attacked in Baltimore County. That's another group of witches and you know that group of reprobates disguised as a coven won't give a damn. Besides, most of my coven are on a retreat cruise in the Bahamas. They won't be back for a week. You'll have to handle this with your own resources, Princess. I can do nothing else for you."

The air of dismissal wafted from her last sentence and Rose paused before giving another nodded bow. I repeated the gesture and followed Rose out. The inner door shut behind me without my assistance.

Back in the Firebird, I waited while Rose backed out and returned to the main road outside the trailer park before I said anything. "Did she give you enough to go on? She wasn't very helpful."

"Jessica was once very beautiful, Chip. Then she dabbled in some very strong magic to expand her power. It worked but left her as you saw her. She's incredibly powerful, but can barely stand up, let alone go anywhere to use that power." Rose chewed on her lower lip for a few seconds. "I hope Warren will be able to track down these Dark Travelers. If he can, we can use them to get to Terrence and rescue Sadie. We'll go as soon as I drop you off at home."

"Gareth should be able to pray for a location on Terrence again in the morning," I said. "Wait until then to go after them. You two shouldn't go alone. You don't know how many there will be."

Rose shook her head. "I'm not letting Sadie spend another night with that monster. If we can get to her now, then we will do our best to try and rescue her."

I wanted to volunteer to go with her, but we both knew I needed at least a night's rest before I'd be up to any sort of fight. It didn't make me feel better to know she'd go out there without me tonight. If they could get Sadie back, then it would be worth my hurt feelings and then some.

"Go and get her back, Rose. If anyone can do it, it's you and Warren."

"I hope you're right, Chip. Our girl needs to be home in her own bed."

Rose

Warren made a few calls while I got Chip inside the house. He and Gareth made plans for the following day while I waited for the werewolf to put his network of contacts to good use. It didn't take him long at all.

"The Dark Travelers hang out in a bar just across the county line," Warren announced. He slipped his phone back into his pocket. "I know exactly where it is. I pass it on the way to visit my sister over in Frederick."

"Will they still be open when we get there?" I asked. "It's after eleven now. It'll be midnight by the time we get there."

"They're open until two so things should just be ramping up for the night." Warren smiled. "If we're lucky, they'll already be pretty drunk. That'll make it easier to beat Terrence's location out of them." Warren cracked his knuckles and let his canines show. His eyes glowed yellow.

Chip said, "Be careful. If you can figure out where they're holding Sadie, we don't need Terrence right away. The focus is on getting her back."

"Understood, Chip," I said. "Warren's just preparing himself for a fight if we need one." I nodded at Warren. "You ready?"

"Let's go."

Gareth said, "You could use another blade in this fight. Take me with you."

I looked at Chip. "You going to be okay here by yourself?"

"I'll be fine. They already have Sadie. I don't see them coming back here for anything else. I'm going to bed to try and heal up. Bring her home, Rose."

"I will. I need to get you a blade, Gareth, if we're going to bring you along. You any good with a sword? All you had was that silver dagger when we first met. We have a few options in the collection."

"Show me what you have," Gareth replied with a twinkle in his eyes. "I can find something serviceable. I killed Terrence once with that enchanted dagger, but another blade will do as well."

I stopped. "What did you say? Terrence is already dead?"

"I remember killing him right before I appeared here," Gareth said. "I stabbed him through the heart and watched him take his last breath."

Chip jumped in before I could. "He's not dead anymore. You said Sadie manifested his ghost in corporeal form. He had to be dead first to be a ghost, right?"

I looked at Gareth. "You think he rose as one of the undead when Sadie brought him here?"

"It's possible. It would explain how he walks the earth after I damned his soul for eternity."

"We'll find out for sure when we catch up with him," I replied. "Either way, he needs killing again. Come on, you two. We've got a gang of rogue warlocks to track down. Chip, I'm taking the minivan in case we get Sadie back. We'll stop by my car to pick up weapons."

"Have fun storming the castle, Rose, and be careful."

"I will."

Warren and Gareth followed me out to the Firebird. I retrieved my sword from behind my seat, grabbing the sheathed long sword in one hand while I dug in my pocket for the keys to unlock the trunk. I walked around to the rear and opened the back. I flipped back the carpet on the false floor to reveal my weapons locker. Inside were several swords and daggers of various types plus a pair of custom-forged tomahawks.

Gareth leaned over to get a good look at the collection. He brushed a hand across the tomahawks for a second then moved on. He pursed his lips in consideration when his hand stopped over a short cutlass with a shiny brass guard.

"That's a good choice," I said. "Small, quick, and its blade is razor sharp."

Gareth nodded. He gripped the cutlass' hilt and pulled it free from the customized slot in the trunk. The witch hunter gave a few practice slashes in the light of the taillights before nodding approval.

"This will do nicely. Thank you for trusting me with a proper weapon."

"Just don't do anything to make me regret that decision. I don't want to have to take it back from you." I ignored his scowl and closed the trunk.

Gareth said, "Doesn't Warren need one, too?"

Warren's eyes flashed yellow in the night. "I come with my own built-in weapons."

I double checked the trunk lid, pushing down until I was sure the latch had clicked. "Let's go."

The pair followed me to the minivan parked in the driveway. I got in the driver's seat. Warren rode shotgun with Gareth perched in the middle of the bench seat right between the kid's car seats.

"Buckle up, gentlemen. I don't drive slowly."

The minivan's six-cylinder engine revved as I punched the accelerator. We peeled out from the driveway and drove down the deserted streets of the development. It was almost eleven-thirty on a weeknight and everyone without a mission like ours was already in bed.

It took forty minutes to drive to the stretch of road in the countryside between Carroll and Frederick Counties. Warren had his GPS open and guided me until we reached a small crossroads. On one corner was an old gas station and on the opposite side was a run-down bar with a neon sign over the door. I pulled over near the closed gas station to watch the bar.

"Tylor's," as it was called, looked like it was hopping. Pickup trucks and motorcycles filled the parking lot and loud music blared forth every time someone went in or out of the front door.

"Perfect," I said. "We'll go in the back. A group like the Dark Travelers won't be hanging in the bar proper. They've got to have somewhere private to conduct their magical ventures."

Warren said, "I could go in and look around first. With my leather jacket, I can blend in with the people we've seen going in and out so far."

"Fine," I said. "But be quick about it. Gareth and I will go around to find the rear entrance. Text me if you find anything worth circling back to the front."

Warren nodded and climbed out. He jogged across the deserted road and walked up to the bar's entrance. He looked back over his shoulder at us, nodded, and then went inside.

"Come on. Time to get moving. Keep that cutlass down at your side. People aren't used to seeing folks walking around with swords in this day and age."

Gareth smiled. "The people of this time have grown soft. They are easy prey for those such as yourself to trick them into following a path to destruction."

I swung around on him behind the minivan with my sword leveled at his chest. "Hey, we're not going to have a problem here, are we? You agreed to help us recover Terrence and find my niece. Are you going back on the arrangement?"

"No, it was merely an observation. I look forward to recovering your niece and getting back to my own time and place."

"Where the men are men and the sheep are fearful," I muttered as I walked away. If he heard me, he didn't reply.

We circled around to the bar's rear. The kitchen and delivery entrance had a plain screen door covering the opening. The inner door was open to let some of the cool night air inside the hot workspace. Gareth and I crouched in the shadows under some poplar trees at the edge of a farm field.

I pulled out my phone as it buzzed.

I've seen several of the Dark Travelers picking up drinks at the bar. They take them back through a side door and down a hallway to the back just like you said.

"That's Warren," I whispered. "He's spotted them. They're inside at the back. You ready?"

Gareth smiled, showing his teeth in the moonlight. I took it as confirmation and stood. I was about to step from the shadows when I spotted Terrence and six coven members walking from the rear entrance. I almost didn't recognize him. He wore blue jeans and a denim jacket.

The witch hunter beside me tensed. He recognized his quarry instantly.

"I'll take Terrence, Gareth. You keep the warlocks busy until Warren gets here to help you."

"Not if I get to him first."

Before I could stop him, Gareth shouted and ran from our hiding place straight at Terrence and the others.

"I have you now, warlock! Prepare for your end, once and for all."

Terrence's head whipped around, and his eyes widened in surprise at seeing Gareth running at him.

The cutlass came down at Terrence's head and I was sure he'd be killed before we could learn Sadie's location. Then the warlock shouted a word of power.

"Still!"

The word came only from Terrence's mouth, but it had the sound of a chorus of many voices behind it. Gareth's body stiffened with his sword raised to strike at the warlock. Then he toppled forward, unable to reach out and catch himself.

"Shit." I charged out after him, trying to get there before one of the Dark Travelers pulled out their curved daggers to finish off the witch hunter. I hoped Warren heard the commotion and came to help. There was no time to text him.

The tattoo-faced men rushed forward with daggers drawn and I knew I'd never get to Gareth in time. Then Terrence held up a hand and the advancing warlocks stopped. I slowed my charge and stopped ten feet away with my sword at my side.

"Hello, Rose. It is a surprise seeing you here with this monster. I expected you to leave him to rot in some modern prison."

"What can I say? Necessity makes for strange bedfellows."

Terrence grinned. "Shakespeare's original quotation from the Tempest is 'Misery acquaints a man with strange bedfellows.' I remember seeing the original production back when I was a much younger Fae rubbing shoulders with the masses of humanity outside Londontown. Still, I understand your meaning."

"You're far older than I originally believed. Now where's Sadie? You better not have laid a hand on her."

"I'm no beast like this one." He kicked out with his booted foot and nudged the rigid body of the witch hunter lying at his feet. "I wouldn't do anything to injure a girl with such power. In fact, I may have plans for her as she ascends to her full strength in the coming years. It depends on how strong she is now."

I let out an angry chuckle. "You think you're going to live long enough to be around to see her ascend to the throne? You'll be lucky to live out the night." I watched the rear exit from the bar out of the corner of my eye, hoping I'd see a werewolf charge out to take all the warlocks from behind. I needed to stall for time.

Terrence smiled. "I think you've mistaken who has the position of power here. You Fae in this century have become soft in your ways living docile lives alongside the humans. These sheep would destroy you if they knew you existed." He pointed down at Gareth's body at his feet and gestured to his followers. "Put him in the van. I think he'll serve as a sacrifice to draw forth the girl's power when the time comes."

"You won't get away with this!" I shouted. "Chip and I'll come for you. You can't run far enough to get away from us."

A pair of warlocks came forward and lifted Gareth under his arms. They carried him to a small, black commercial van parked nearby. The remaining Dark Travelers backed away towards the vehicle with the others. That left Terrence and I facing each other.

"Tell the Guardian that I have clouded his vision of the queen permanently. He will not find her with his paltry powers. I will let the two of you live. There may be a need for you both to remain alive for the time being. But do not test me further, princess. If I see either of the two of you again, I will kill you both and find another way to exercise my plan."

The van started and the Dark Travelers piled in the back. One waited, holding one of the rear doors open, waiting for Terrence. I couldn't let him get away.

Drawing in power, I applied the energy in a magical burst of speed forward, leading with my sword in a lunge. Terrence didn't even dodge my thrust.

The blade entered the center of his chest, and I stopped standing up straight with my arm extended.

Terrence looked down at the sword in his chest and then back up at me with a smile on his face.

How was he still alive?

He showed his teeth and reached out, wrapping both hands around my fingers where they held my sword's hilt. With slow and steady strength, he pulled me forward. The sword slid into his chest all the way up to the cross guard, stopping against his shirt. It was then I noticed there was no blood.

"What are you?" I asked.

Face to face, his fetid breath made me cough.

His lips peeled back in a vicious grin. "Something not seen in this world for over two hundred years. Good night, Rose."

He tipped his head back and brought it forward so fast I couldn't dodge away. His forehead slammed into my nose. Stars exploded across my vision. The last thing I remembered was Terrence prying my hand from my sword's hilt. Then it all went black as I fell backward.

I screamed in the darkness, struggling to push back towards the light that seemed just out of reach. I don't know how long I tried to wade through the darkness, but it felt like an eternity.

"Rose, gods-dammit, why didn't you wait?" Someone shook me. "Wake up, Rose. We need to get out of here."

My eyes fluttered open. Warren's face floated a few inches away from mine. The words I needed to speak came slowly. "T-t-terrance? Where is he?"

"I don't know. I came out and you were lying here alone in the gravel lot behind the bar next to your sword. Where's Gareth? Did he do this to you?"

My brain throbbed like it wanted to explode from my skull. I pushed through the pain and worked to focus my eyes to search beyond

Warren's face. I was right where he said I was. The rear of the bar was right there. What wasn't there was the van full of warlocks.

"Shit, they got away. Warren, we have to follow them."

"Follow who?" Warren looked around. "There's no one back here."

"There was the same black van. They took Gareth and left me here unconscious." I pulled away from Warren's grasp and stumbled to my feet.

"Careful, Rose. You were out for a few minutes. Come on over to the minivan and sit down."

"No, we have to find them." I bent over and picked up my sword from the gravel. The blade was sticky with something that wasn't quite blood.

"We're not finding anyone tonight, Rose. They're gone. We'll have to find another way. I have to take you to a doctor to get looked at. Your face is a mess."

I let him lead me back around the bar and over to the side of the minivan parked across the road. I could see myself in the reflection of the intersection's lone streetlight in the window. My swollen nose filled the center of my view, and I had two black eyes. Blood had smeared across my entire face and had flowed back to dry in a crust in my hair. It was hard to admit it, but Warren was right.

"Let's go. Take me back to Chip's. We'll regroup back there."

"You need a doctor, Rose." Warren said.

"I've had worse. I'll rest while you drive. We'll reassess when I get back to the house."

I climbed into the passenger seat and handed Warren the keys from my pocket. I barely remembered him pulling out of the lot. All my brain wanted to do was to sleep and I gave in to it. There wasn't anything else I could do. I'd lost our chance to get Sadie back.

18

Chip

I woke up after just a few hours of sleep to a commotion downstairs. I thought maybe they'd returned with Sadie. I pulled on sweatpants and a t-shirt and ran down the stairs, ignoring the pounding headache behind my eyes.

"Let go of me," Rose hissed. "I'm not an invalid."

Warren replied with, "You nearly fell over when I stopped to close the garage door. Let me help you."

I turned the corner at the bottom of the steps. Warren held onto Rose's arm while she lowered herself into a spot on the end of the sofa. Despite her complaints, she gripped his other arm with her free hand to keep from falling over.

"What happened?" I asked. My head swiveled, taking in the room. "Where's Sadie?"

"We didn't find her, Chip," Rose said. "Terrence got the drop on us. He— he's not what we thought he was."

"He's a true undead. Like a vampire, but maybe worse," Warren said. "He has to be to do what you said he did."

"What did you do?"

"I ran him through with my sword and he head butted me before running away."

"That explains your face," I said. "Jeeze, Rose. You're a bloody mess. At least you injured him."

She shook her head. "I don't know if I did."

I didn't understand. "But you said—"

"I know what I said. I ran him through, and he ignored it. He even laughed like it was nothing but a scratch, a mere flesh wound."

"How?" I still struggled with what she was describing.

"What Warren said is right. He's some form of undead, but I need to do more research to find out what he might be exactly. It's important that we know for sure if we're going to take him on."

Warren shrugged. "I didn't think Fae could become undead. I thought it wasn't a thing."

"Oh, it's a thing alright." Rose reached up to touch her nose with a finger and glanced at it. "Shit, I'm bleeding again. Someone get me a towel."

Both Warren and I moved towards the bathroom.

She snarled and pushed up from the sofa's arm. "Never mind. Help me to the bathroom. I need to look in a mirror and do this myself."

I put a hand under her elbow to steady her. Warren took up station on the other side. We went around the stairs and down the hall to the small powder room. She pulled one of the blue hand towels from the bar inside the door and held it under the faucet while she turned on the water.

I stood in the doorway and watched while she dabbed at the crusted blood around her nose and mouth. I couldn't recall seeing her beat up this much. I hoped it didn't scar her face permanently. She'd probably say it added character. For me, it would serve as a reminder that I should have been there with her.

Her eyes met mine through the mirror. "I can do this myself, thank you." She reached back and swung the door closed as I backed into the hallway.

Warren and I walked back out to the family room to wait for her to come out. He grimaced.

"They could've killed her, Chip. They left her alive for some reason, for which I should thank the gods. I wasn't there to back her up in time."

"She wasn't alone, right? Gareth was with her." I stopped. "Hey, where's Gareth?"

"They took him with them. That's more of the puzzle. Rose isn't sure why, but she thinks they're going to stage some sort of ritual killing with him at the center of it."

"We can't let that happen," I said. "Did you at least figure a way to track them down?"

Warren frowned. "How? They got away with Gareth and left Rose unconscious. I didn't see any of it. I don't even know which way they went."

I'd never seen Warren like this before. He wasn't usually a defeatist kind of guy. I shifted my voice to a firmer tone. "Hey, that's enough of that. You may not like the outcome tonight. I don't like it either. But it's not like you to give up. Get ahold of yourself."

Warren took a deep breath and squared his shoulders. After a few seconds, he said, "Thanks. I needed that."

"No problem. Now, what do we know?"

Warren paced back and forth in front of the sofa before he said. "They got away in a black commercial van. It sounds like the one they used at the restaurant. Rose said there were no markings on it, so it might be a rental."

I smiled. "That's gotta narrow down things a little, right? How many places rent black commercial vans like that around here? It's not like we're in the city."

Warren kept pacing in silence a little longer. "I need to follow up on that and some of the other clues. Can you watch over her? I'm worried about how she's doing."

"I've got Rose, you go and do your detective thing. Get back to us when you have a lead."

The werewolf left with a definite, purposeful spring in his step as he went out the front door. I closed it behind him.

"Where's he going?"

I jumped a little, startled by Rose's voice right behind me. She'd snuck up on me again. "He's going to track down a black van. He needed something to occupy his mind." I turned to face her. "He's worried about you and thinks he let you down."

"That's nonsense," Rose said. "I'm a big girl. I knew the risks attacking a group of warlocks like that."

I smiled as she moved into the light out of the shadows. Her face looked a little better with all the dried blood washed away. Maybe not much better, but enough that I wasn't worried she might be dying.

"Why are you looking at me like that? Stop it. I don't need you going all man-hero on me. That's not us."

I laughed. "Sorry, I was thinking how bad you looked before you got cleaned up."

She laughed with me for a second. "I was a mess." She stopped and frowned. "But my face is nothing. They still have Sadie, Chip. We have to keep working to get her back."

"I gave Warren something to do. He'll find out where they are. What do we do in the meantime?"

Rose returned to sit on the sofa and lay back so she stared up at the ceiling. "I can't believe I'm saying this, but we need to go to the Seer."

"Who's that?"

"It's more like 'what's that?' The Seer is unlike the rest of us. They aren't human, or Fae, or anything else recognizable. They just are."

"Okay, where do we find them?" I asked. "I don't care who or what they might be. If they can help us find our girl, then I'm all in."

"I'm not sure. That's the problem. They're located somewhere in Elk City, but I've never heard of a single location. It's a closely guarded secret. Every story I've heard has been different. It's as if they move around from place to place to avoid people."

"If I was the one with all the answers and people knew I existed, I might avoid everyone, too." I laughed a little and added, "Okay, where do we start?"

"How comfortable are you reaching out to that weird vampire cousin of yours? He lives in Elk City and might have a connection we can use to get to the seer."

"Gibbie?" I asked with a chuckle. "I can call him if you think it'll help. We've corresponded a few times since we ran into him in that club in Baltimore. I'm sure he'll want to help. He's all about family."

"Good, you get ahold of him. Tell him we need to see the Seer and need it right now. Make your cousin understand how important this is."

I nodded. "I can do that, though he's more of a distant uncle than a cousin, at least technically."

When I didn't pull out my phone right away, Rose stared at me until I said, "I'll get right on it first thing in the morning."

"Do it now, Chip. He's a vampire. Morning is his bedtime."

I realized she was right. "Oh, yeah. You're right. Okay, I'm on it." His contact information was in my phone, and I composed a simple text message to him, trying to get to the point without being pushy. I didn't want him to say no.

Hey, Gibbie. I wondered if you knew how to hook up a guy with the Seer in Elk City?

The message sent and he must have seen it immediately as the indicator on the screen showed he was replying. I waited for his answer.

What do you want them for, Chip? They don't fool around.

I hesitated for only a second before I let my reasons go. Gibbie was family. He'd want to know and help in any way he could.

Someone kidnapped Sadie and we need help tracking them down to get her back.

A red exclamation point emoji followed with a text message right behind it.

Why didn't you lead with that, Chip? Of course I'll help. Wait for my call.

I put down my phone and sighed. I hoped Gibbie could assist. He came off as a bit of a screwup sometimes.

"Well?" Rose asked when I shoved the phone in my pocket.

"I got him. He's tracking the Seer down and will reach out when he has a lead."

"How much did you tell him?"

"Everything, Rose. He has a right to know. Sadie's related to him, too."

She frowned. "He'll want to know what's so important about a nine-year-old girl to a kidnapper. It won't take much to put her real identity together if he starts digging."

I held up a hand to stop her accusations. "Proctors stick together, Rose. You don't need to worry about Gibbie. He'll come through."

My phone buzzed in my pocket with an incoming call. I checked and saw it was Gibbie. I showed the screen to Rose and then swiped to open the call and put it on speaker.

"Gibbie, tell me some good news."

"I found the Seer."

I smiled. "That was fast. I expected you to take a few hours."

"I have connections in very high places. There's a problem, though."

Rose stepped forward. "What kind of problem? We need to talk to the Seer right away."

"Is that Rose?" Gibbie asked. His low laugh carried over the connection. "You two finally together now? I could tell there was a vibe between you the last time we met."

"No! Nothing like that," I replied before Rose could snap an angry answer. "Focus, Gibbie. Stick to the Seer thing. What is the problem with them?"

"They're leaving town tomorrow morning. You have to see them tonight or they'll be gone for a month. Are you in Westminster?"

I said, "We are. We can be there in an hour and a half."

Gibbie paused before replying. I could hear another voice in the background, but it was muffled as if he was covering the microphone while he conferred with them.

"Okay, that should be enough time. My friend will let them know you're coming. Hurry up, Chip. The Seer isn't the type to just hang around and wait for people."

"We're leaving now," Rose said. "Where should we meet you?"

"What about Addy?" I asked. "We can't leave him here by himself."

"We'll take him with us. Go wake him up. I'll get the location from Gibbie."

I handed the phone to Rose and ran upstairs while she finished the call and got the address for our rendezvous.

Addy stared up at me, confusion in his little eyes. "It's dark, Uncle Chip. Why are you getting me up in the middle of the night?"

"We're going on a surprise trip. Come on and get dressed. We have to leave right now."

He sat up and rubbed at the sleep in his eyes with his closed fists. I got him some pants, a T-shirt, and a sweatshirt. It was chilly out this time of year. I took his hand, and we went downstairs. Rose was nowhere to be seen, but I heard the motor for the garage door running through the kitchen door.

We walked to the entrance to the garage. Rose already sat behind the wheel of the minivan. "Get in, Chip. We need to get on the road."

I loaded up Addy in his booster seat and climbed into the passenger seat. "Should you drive? You probably have a concussion."

"So do you. You can drive back if you want. We need to go now, and I drive faster than you."

A little voice in the back of my mind said, *yeah, and you drive crazier than me, too.* I left that part unsaid and leaned back in my seat as Rose gunned the engine and headed for the highway. We were Elk City bound.

19

Rose

On the way to Elk City, I explained the rules for asking a Seer questions, at least as I understood them. I'd never actually encountered one before. The rules were simple, though. We'd have a limited number of requests to present, perhaps only one. We had to phrase our question in a way that would mine the most information in a single response. Asking a yes or no question would get a single word answer. We needed to get the Seer to tell us as much as possible from their vision of the answer to the question. Chip and I rolled through some variations of our central question. Where was Sadie and how do we get her back? It was technically two questions, but we'd refine it on our drive.

By the time we arrived in Elk City, it was nearly four in the morning. Addy had fallen back to sleep in the rear of the minivan. I checked the GPS on my phone as we drove downtown in Elk City. When it showed we'd arrived at our destination I leaned forward to stare at the tall, sleek building outside the van.

"This doesn't look like the kind of place that weird cousin of yours would live, Chip. Is he secretly wealthy and we don't know it?"

"I don't think so." Chip pulled out his phone. "I'm the only rich Proctor as far as I know. Let me call him."

I waited, pulled over in a no parking zone in front while he made the call.

"Gibbie? It's Chip. Yeah, we're here. Do we go in the front door? It looks like it's closed up for the night."

Chip paused, listening. "Okay, we'll be right there." Chip glanced at me and pointed ahead. "Drive around the block until we reach the entrance to the underground garage. He'll meet us there. The guard is expecting us."

I did as Chip instructed and went around back until I saw the ramp leading down beneath the building. The sign read "Nightwing Building Employees, Residents, and Guests Only."

A guard, who I was pretty sure was a werewolf, checked my ID at the gate and then stepped back to raise the bar so we could drive in.

Chip pointed down the ramp. "Gibbie said to go down to the elevators on the second level."

I drove around looking for the ramp down. Most of the parking spaces were empty. I turned down to the second level and spotted Gibbie over by a bank of elevators. He waved and pointed to a spot across from him. I pulled in next to a beat-up white Chevy van.

"Addy, time to wake up," Chip said. "We're here."

"Where? Did you find Sadie?" The kid looked around, blinking in the bright lights of the underground garage.

"No, but we're looking for her real hard, right, Rose?"

I nodded. "Don't you worry, Addy. We'll find your sister. Now hop out of your seat and let's go see your cousin Gibbie."

Addy brightened up and jumped down out of the side of the van. "Gibbie!" He wrapped his arms around the surprised vampire's legs.

Gibbie patted Addy on the head. "Hey, there, kiddo. You're getting so big. I just saw you a year ago and you were barely up to here." He held a hand out to Addy's shoulder.

"I'm growing up. Soon, I'll be the one to guard Sadie. No one will take her away then."

Gibbie looked up at me. "Yeah, what's up with that? You need help? You know you just have to ask, and I'll rally the troops."

I jumped in. "We'll let you know if we need more help. Right now, Chip and I are working on it." I had no idea who a screw-up vampire like Chip's cousin would find to help us in a situation like this. I was surprised he knew how to contact the Seer at all. I'd prefer we kept the search for Sadie in-house as much as possible. I smiled and said, "It's a big help that you were able to locate the Seer for us. How, exactly, did you do that?"

"I had to call in a favor, but for family it's all worth it. Come on. Let's go upstairs. I have someone for you to meet. She's the one who knows where the Seer is."

We all piled into the elevator and up we went. Gibbie surprised me when he punched the button labeled "PH" for the penthouse level. Maybe he had means and access after all.

The elevator opened onto a professionally decorated entry hall with a single door at the end. Gibbie gestured for us to follow him. He walked up to the door and knocked.

We waited about thirty seconds before the door opened to reveal a tall, very attractive redhead in a tight skirt, white blouse, and a blazer. Judging from her pale skin, this one was a vamp as well. She stepped back and waved us inside a very nice, upscale apartment.

"Celeste, these are the people I told you about. This is my cousin Chip and his friend Rose. And this little one is Addy."

Celeste frowned. "Going to visit the Seer is no place for a kid, Gibbie. You should know that."

Chip said, "That's my fault. We couldn't leave him home alone and our matter is quite urgent. He'll be on his best behavior, right, Addy?"

"You got it, Uncle Chip." The little guy gave Celeste a thumbs up.

Celeste stared at Addy for an uncomfortable five seconds, then sniffed. "Suit yourselves. I was able to contact the Seer. I called in a favor James owed to the Seer for this, Gibbie. I'll expect you to honor it should we ever need you for a favor of our own."

"Of course, Celeste. You know I'm all about pitching in where I'm needed."

"Good. Now, I've contacted the Seer on your behalf. They're only expecting three of you, though. I can't call back and change that. The boy will have to stay here."

That caught me by surprise. I balked instantly and stepped in front of Addy. "There's no way I'm leaving you a midnight snack, vampire."

Celeste's eyes widened, then instantly narrowed to slits in anger. She took a step in my direction.

I let power fill me, letting the glow of it fill my emerald eyes. I was ready for this fight.

Celeste snarled, her lips curling back to reveal her fangs. "Bring it, sister."

Gibbie jumped in between us just in time. "Ladies, ladies, let's not get off on the wrong foot here." He waited until he was sure we'd both backed away a step and turned to Chip. "I vouch for Celeste, Chip. She'll protect Addy with her life. He won't have so much as a scratch when we come back to pick him up."

Chip looked back and forth between his cousin and the vampire a few times, then said, "Gibbie's right, Rose. If he vouches for her, that's all I need. I'm the Guardian. It's my call. Besides, save that energy for our fight with Terrence. He's the one we should be angry with."

I shook my head. "You're just blinded by her looks, Chip. You're hoping for a date later."

Celeste said with a chuckle as she checked her manicured nails, "Good luck with that. He's definitely not my type at all."

Chip frowned at her instant refusal of him as a prospect and then gathered himself again. "I said it's fine. Besides, we know where she lives. Think about it. If anything happens to Addy, we know how to find her."

"If you say so, Chip. It's your call. But I don't like it." I glared at Celeste. She didn't back down an inch, glaring right back.

It was Chip's turn to step in between us. "Rose, I said I trust Gibbie. We've got to get Sadie back. This is the only way."

Celeste pulled out her phone. "Here's the address, Gibbie. I'll send the instructions to see the Seer while you're on the way there. I didn't know what vehicle they'd be driving, so the Seer is expecting you and your van."

"Sounds good to me," Gibbie said. "I can drive. Shall we go?" He waved a hand back at the hallway to the elevators.

I didn't want to leave Addy here, but Chip was right. We had to trust someone while we went and tracked down Sadie. I glared one last time at Celeste and walked back into the entry hall.

Chip leaned down to Addy. "You be good and listen to Miss Celeste here." He stood up and said, "He's bone tired. Let him lay down on a comfortable chair and put on cartoons and he'll be out for the rest of the night."

"I'll keep that in mind. He'll be fine with me. I swear on my honor. Now, go. The Seer doesn't like to wait."

Gibbie walked past me and punched the elevator button. Chip and I joined him. Behind us, Celeste shut the door.

I stared straight ahead at the elevator doors and said, "I swear, if she lays one hand on that boy, I'll take it out on both of you after I'm finished with her."

Neither Gibbie nor Chip said anything, which was probably a wise move. We rode back down to the garage in silence. Gibbie unlocked the passenger door to his van and opened the slider with his keys, then walked around to the driver's side.

I pointed at Chip to the front seat. This was his cousin. I climbed into the back and closed the sliding door behind me. I grimaced and pushed a stack of empty Redbull cans to the floor and sat down on the bench seat so I could see out between the two front bucket seats.

Gibbie fired up the engine and soon we were back on the streets of Elk City. There were a few more cars on the road now than before, but not that many. People were starting to rise for the early shift jobs. He drove fast through the sparse traffic for about fifteen minutes until we got to a residential neighborhood with very nice homes. He checked his phone and then leaned forward to peer at the passing mailboxes and house numbers.

"This is the one." He pulled into a driveway that looped back around behind a large manor-style home on about one acre of land. He drove over to a small, detached garage with a second story above it and stopped.

"That's the place according to the information Celeste gave me. You're supposed to go up those stairs and knock on the door of the apartment over the garage."

"This all-important Seer lives up there?" Chip asked.

Gibbie shrugged. "Celeste said this is the place. She doesn't lie."

Chip twisted around in his seat and looked back at me. I didn't have anything to say. This was a bit of a surprise to me as well. Seers were incredibly rare. At any given time, there were only about a dozen in the whole world. We were lucky there was even one within driving distance.

"Let's go, Chip," I said. I leaned over and pulled back the sliding door. I hopped down to the driveway beside the van. "Celeste was right about one thing. We don't want to keep the Seer waiting."

He looked back up at the dim lights coming from the apartment and then shook his head. After he hopped out beside me, we both walked to the stairs. Chip waved for me to go first. I took the stairs two at a time. I wanted to get this over with. Chip bounded up the steps behind me.

I rapped on the door with my knuckles and waited for a response. When none came, I leaned down and peered in through the broad window set in the door. I could barely see through the crack in the white curtains hung inside. What I could see was a very large flatscreen TV with a first-person shooter video game in progress on it. The back of a tall, multi-colored, leather upholstered chair on wheels blocked my view of whoever was playing the game.

When there was no sign of the gamer noticing our presence at all, I balled up my fist and banged on the door three times. This time there was a response. A hand came out from behind the chair with its middle finger raised in our direction. A voice called out from inside.

"Wait your fucking turn, asshole."

That was enough of that. It was obvious to me that we'd gotten bad information. This wasn't the Seer at all. I wanted inside to find out exactly how we were being played. I leaned back and raised a booted foot to kick in the wooden door.

Chip grabbed me by the shoulders and yanked me back on the small landing at the top of the wooden stairs. I almost pitched over the railing to the ground below. Chip kept his grip on me, though, and I was able to regain my balance.

"Easy, Rose. Let me try."

"That jerk in there just flipped me off, Chip. I don't think the Seer's even here."

He opened his mouth to answer but stopped when the apartment's door opened. A pimply-faced teenager with short-cropped, purple and pink hair answered the door. They had multiple piercings, including both ears and a silver nose ring. The baggy, long-sleeved clothing left everything else about them up to speculation.

"You two the ones Celeste called about?"

Chip nodded.

"Come inside before you wake up my parents."

Chip grinned back at me and followed the kid inside. I ground my teeth and walked in after him, closing the door. I'd let him take the lead. Otherwise, there was going to be one less snarky teenager around.

20

Chip

Rose grumbled under her breath behind me while we followed the kid into the spacious one-room apartment. A double bed with tousled sheets and blanket sat in the corner opposite us. Beside it was a desk with a three-monitor computer station set up. Next to that was the flat-screen with the game system playing on it and the gamer chair in front. A small kitchenette and round table with four chairs filled out the room nearest the door along with a beat-up fabric sofa facing the flat-screen.

"I don't usually take these appointments on the fly like this," they said, stopping beside the small table. "If it wasn't because of the favor I owed James, I wouldn't have seen you like this."

"I'm sorry, James?" I asked.

"James Lee, the vampire lord of Elk City? You're here because you asked him to reach out to me, right?"

"Uh, yeah, that's right." I thought Celeste was the one who'd set it up, but apparently, she wasn't the bigwig here. She acted like she ran the place, but when I thought back about it, there was an air of the able assistant about her. I've known a dozen or so like her over my years on Wall Street. They were indispensable to their executives and wielded quite a bit of power because of their proximity to the top.

They were also among the most trusted in the inner circle. If she was connected to the top vamp in Elk City, it wouldn't surprise me.

The Seer gestured to the two chairs on the opposite side of the round table from them. Rose and I sat down, and they sat opposite us.

"You two know how this works?"

Rose opened her mouth to speak, but I cut her off. "Why don't you refresh our memories to make sure there are no misconceptions or failed expectations." This wasn't my first negotiation.

"Fine," the Seer said, pulling out a stick of gum and popping it into their mouth. "You each get a question. One, that's it. Any more than that and I'll have a migraine for a week. I'll give you the answer to those questions in the form they come to me and then you leave. I'm in the middle of a tournament and my guild expects me to win it for them." They nodded back at the paused game system against the far wall. "Also, you have to be gone before my parents wake up."

"Okay," I said. "I guess I'll go first. My niece, Sadie, is missing. How do I find her exact location?"

The Seer's eyebrows lowered and then their eyes glowed white. When the light dimmed in the eyes staring back at me, they were pure, milky white. No irises. No pupils. Just white.

"You don't. The one who has her is rotating her through numerous locations. What you can do is trap them into coming to you. That's your only chance."

The Seer stopped talking and turned to face Rose with the blank, white gaze. I knew what her question was. We'd discussed the problems facing us. I hoped she got a better or more thorough answer than I did. I didn't like what I'd been told at all.

"The one who has Sadie is undead, but in a way that I don't recognize. How do I defeat them?"

The young Seer flashed their teeth in a fierce grin. "That's easy. Fight the dead with the dead."

"What does that mean?" Rose asked. She leaned forward and grabbed the Seer's tattooed forearm showing below the loose sleeve. "You have to tell me more."

"One question each. That was the deal." They glanced down at the hand on the forearm. The tattoos flashed red.

Rose hissed in pain. She yanked her hand back. Tendrils of smoke wafted up from her burned palm.

"Okay, we've obviously overstayed our welcome here. Rose, go out to the van. I'll be right there."

"Chip, you heard them. We're finished here."

"I'll be right down," I said. "Promise."

Rose clutched her injured hand to her chest and got up. She walked to the door and left down the stairs.

The Seer stood. "I will not answer any further questions. My arrangement with James Lee has been met."

I nodded at the game paused on the screen. "Is that *Creed of Legends*?"

"It is," The Seer replied. Their eyes had returned to normal. "Why?"

"I'm good friends with the founder of Gaither Games. As a matter of fact, I just heard from her that the new *Creed of Legends II* is ready for a closed Beta."

"Wait, you can get access to the Beta for *Legends II*?"

I nodded. "Is that worth another answer?"

"Damn, you bet it is!" They looked over their shoulder at the game running on the screen, then added, "But only if you can get access for me and all of my guild members."

This was going to cost me a lot of money, but Sadie was worth every penny if it got me the answers I needed.

I smiled. "You and no more than four guild members. Early Beta access through launch. Deal?"

"Abso-fucking-lutely, dude. What's your question?"

"You said I had to lure the kidnapper to a location of my choice. What's the one bait Terrence can't resist?"

"That's easy. I saw it in my earlier vision. There's a silver spike connected directly to the netherworld. It belonged to a demon who left it here on earth when they were vanquished during the crusades."

"I don't have time to search the globe for a missing silver spike."

"You don't have to search. It's in your girlfriend's family collection." The Seer pointed to the door where Rose had just left.

"Rose isn't my girlfriend."

The Seer grinned and winked. "Believe what you want. You'll see."

I ignored the kid's games about Rose. "What is it about this spike that's important?"

The kid laughed. "That's another question, but for *Legends II* Beta access, it's worth the headache." The eyes flashed again and went white. After a pause, the Seer said, "Terrence will use the spike to damn the witch hunter's soul to hell at the same instant he collects your niece's power. Lure him with that and he'll show up."

Their eyes faded back to their original state and the Seer took a step to the side. They raised a hand to their head and grimaced. "Go, I still need to finish the game and this migraine is going to play hell with my gaming skills for a while."

I nodded and left them there in the middle of the apartment. Rose waited in the van for me. A light rain had started, and I ran down the stairs to jump in the passenger seat.

Gibbie smiled as he drove away. "Did you get what you needed? Rose said she got a half answer."

"I found out what we needed to know. At least, I know how to get Terrence to come to us. I have no idea how to defeat him, though." I twisted in my seat to look back at Rose. "I hope you've been able to make sense of the answer you got."

"I have some ideas, but none of them are good. Let's go pick up Addy and head back to Westminster." As Gibbie drove through the early morning grayness, Rose asked, "What did you talk about when you sent me out? Were you able to get anything else out of them?"

"Yes."

Gibbie's eyes went wide. "You got an extra question out of the Seer. Nobody does that. I gotta say, Chip. That's epic. They're supposed to be immune to all forms of persuasion and torture. Not that I think you'd use torture. I'm just saying."

I smiled and leaned back in the seat, putting a foot up on the dash. "What can I say? Once a prime Wall Street trader and dealmaker, always a prime Wall Street trader and dealmaker. I had something worth more than the Seer's rules. Once I made it known to them, they jumped at the chance to answer one more question."

"What did you do, Chip?" Rose asked. She sneered. "You didn't sell your soul or something stupid like that, did you?"

"It'll cost me my controlling interest in a very lucrative investment in my portfolio. It's all okay if it gets us Sadie back. I found out what we need to flush out Terrence."

Rose leaned forward. "What's that?"

"Some magical silver demon spike your family has. Terrence knows about it and wants to use it to both banish Gareth and harvest Sadie's power."

"Silver sp—" Rose's eyes widened in surprise. "Ba'al's Lance. It has to be."

"Who?" Gibbie asked.

"Ba'al is a demon who terrorized whole swaths of central Europe during the early Dark Ages. The church sent a legion of paladin knights against him. They defeated him, but before he died, he used his strength to cast his lance far from the battlefield into the densely forested mountains around them. They searched for a long time, but never found it."

I smiled. I saw the answer in her tale. "That's because a certain Fae family discovered it first and squirreled it away to keep its power from the bad humans. Right?"

"It has long been a practice of Fae nobility to hold weapons and talismans of great power so humanity's leaders don't abuse the magics they contain."

"Great, Rose, so you know where it is?" I asked.

"Yes, it's at Aunt Allura's. But she's never going to let us take it from the secure vault beneath her home. It's safe there."

I shook my head. "No, it's not. Think about it. Terrence is a member of your family. He probably came over with your family's original settlers to the new world. He has to know about all the items in the ancestral collection. He'll attack Allura to retrieve it. Our only chance is to use it to trick him to come to us at a time and place of our choosing."

"It won't help us if I can't figure out what the Seer told me." Rose said. "It's a puzzle. Only the dead can kill the dead? What's that all about?"

I laughed. "That one is easy. We need a necromancer."

Rose snapped her fingers. "Yes, of course. But how are we going to lay our hands on one? They don't advertise online, you know."

"Didn't we just chase one off a few weeks ago?" I asked. "We never caught them. Maybe they're still around."

"I'm sure they took the hint and got out of the area. We haven't heard any more rumors of insane zombies running around."

I considered what she said, but it didn't make sense. "Rose, the Seer told us what we needed and, in every other case, the advice related to something we already had in our possession or had access to. That has to mean the necromancer is still in the area. Maybe they're not so smart after all and stuck around."

Gibbie had arrived at the Nightwing Building and drove down into the underground garage. He led us back up to the Penthouse. We heard voices and laughter from outside the door.

"That's Addy," Rose said. "Didn't we tell her to get him to sleep?"

"Relax, Rose," I said. "At least she didn't kill him like you thought she would."

"I heard that." Celeste had opened the door before any of us could ring the bell. "The kid's fun. I never had a desire to birth one, even when I was human, but Addy is okay, as far as little kids go."

THWAK!

The sound turned all our heads to the left as we entered. Addy had just thrown a tomahawk to embed into the center of a large wooden target mounted on the wall at the far side of the room.

"Look, Celeste! I did it!"

"Yes, you did. You keep practicing that and you'll become very good with one of those someday."

Addy's eyes lit up. "I can keep it?"

"Sure, kid. The Boss'll never miss it. He has too many weapons in the armory to keep track of."

Addy jumped up with a fist pump and ran to the target. It took him a little work, but he managed to wiggle the embedded tomahawk free. "Look, Uncle Chip. I have my very own throwing axe."

"I see that." I laughed at his glee.

"It's a tomahawk, Addy," Rose said. She nodded to the vampire. "What do you say to Miss Celeste?"

"Thank you, Miss Celeste. I'll never forget this."

"See that you don't," the redhead replied with a grin. "I hope you all got the information you needed?"

Gibbie said, "They got an extra question out of the Seer. Isn't that awesome?"

"Really?" Her eyebrows rose in surprise. "That's quite unusual."

"What can I say?" I replied. "I'm an unusual kind of guy." I winked at Celeste and reached out for Addy's free hand. He cradled the tomahawk close to his chest with his other. "Come on, Addy. Time to go and let Miss Celeste get some rest. It's almost daytime."

"Gibbie will show you out. I have a few calls to make to Europe before I settle in for the day." She walked away into the Penthouse.

We followed Gibbie back to the elevator and down to the parking garage. It was time to get home and see about saving Sadie from Terrence. On instinct, I reached out for her, searching for the familiar link that had been all but severed. I got the now-familiar distant sense of her general well-being but couldn't localize it the way I used to. At least I knew she was alive. It would be up to Rose and me to make sure she stayed that way and we got her back.

Rose

I had two very different problems on my plate in order to get Sadie back. The first was to figure a way to get into the vault beneath Aunt Allura's manor house without her knowing I'd been there. I was pretty sure there'd be wards on something as important and powerful as Ba'al's Lance. I had a pretty good idea that Terrence would want to get his hands on the lance sooner than later. The dark midnight of the new moon was a few days off and that was a night of great power with evil artifacts. That couldn't be a coincidence.

The other problem, besides the time concerns, centered around locating a necromancer powerful enough to overcome Terrence and his obvious power and ability. It couldn't be some random magic user who dabbled in necromancy among other things. This required someone who had a proven record of raising and controlling undead bodies. Someone like the necromancer we ran off a few weeks before.

As it turned out, Chip was right about the necromancer we'd tracked before. He might still be in the area. I hated to admit it, but when I had Warren check around, the necromancer we'd chased away from the farm had used their debit card at the local Costco the day before. That couldn't be a coincidence. He had stuck around despite us rooting him out of his lair in that old home.

I would have to go alone to search for him. Warren was still trying to track down Terrence and the Dark Travelers' location. Chip had his hands full keeping an eye on Addy, who was very worried about his sister. That kid was shaping up to be a full-time job all by himself. He was acting out and misbehaving in reaction to everyone else's tension and anxiety.

Addison had gotten in trouble in school the day after we got back from the Seer's trip. He snuck the tomahawk into his backpack for show and tell that day. When he took it out to show his classmates and teacher, he demonstrated how he could throw it. Addy embedded it in the door a few inches from the principal's face who had just peeked in to check on the classroom.

I almost smiled at the image it brought to mind. Addy was growing up to be a formidable warrior, which he should be as the protector of the future queen. Of course, raising him to adulthood was going to be a special challenge, but that was the Guardian's problem, wasn't it?

With nowhere else to start, I decided to begin the search for the necromancer at the Costco. On the way there, I placed a call to my aunt to sound her out about the family collection of artifacts and relics. Maybe I could discover a way to convince her to let us borrow the lance for a few days. It was worth a shot. I hadn't been able to come up with any better ideas.

Reston, my aunt's butler, answered the phone. Aunt Allura still refused to get a cell phone. The only way to reach her was through her old, copper-wired landline and phone.

"Princess Rose, how may I be of assistance to you?"

I put on my sweetest voice and said, "I need to talk with my aunt. Is she available?"

"May I ask what this is about?"

"I hadn't checked in recently about Sadie and Addy and I wanted to give her an update on their training, if you must know."

"Hmmm."

Did I detect a hint of disbelief there?

"Is she available or not?"

"I'm afraid the mistress left town suddenly on short notice. A dear friend of hers had a sudden injury and died. She left for New York this afternoon."

"Gee," I muttered, "it would've been nice to get a heads up."

"The mistress is quite busy, Princess. She doesn't have time to update you on all her comings and goings. After all, you don't apprise her of your every move, do you?"

He wasn't wrong, but it also wasn't like her to whisk herself away on short notice like this. Given everything that was going on, a suspicious person might wonder if there was a connection back to Terrence.

"Reston, what exactly happened to this friend of hers?"

"It was quite tragic. A rogue band of humans on motorcycles ran her car off the road and robbed her. They killed her after relieving her of her jewels and money. It was all very unusual for the area from what I understand."

"Do the human authorities have any clues about who did it?"

Reston said, "Nothing concrete based on the brief conversation I had with the mistress."

I couldn't help but wonder if the bikers in question wore the colors of the Dark Travelers. This might be Terrence's way of clearing access to the family vault. Allura possessed powerful magic of her own and wasn't without her defenses or retainers. This had to mean he planned to come on the dark midnight in two days.

A thought came to me. "What are the plans for the house with her gone for a while?"

"Ms. McGarry and I plan to take the weekend off for a much-needed break, if you must know. The stableman will be on the property to take care of the horses, but the house will be closed up until she returns next Tuesday."

"I think it's a great idea that you and Ms. McGarry take a few days for yourselves. Good for you, Reston. Here I thought you were all work and no play."

"Indeed. You'll be surprised to hear I write mystery novels in my spare time. There is an event one of my author friends is holding this weekend in Atlanta, and I'm going down to participate on short notice."

"I shouldn't have doubted you, Reston. Have a good trip."

"You have a good weekend, too, Princess. Goodbye."

He hung up the phone and I cursed to myself. This had to be something Terrence had orchestrated. We had less time than expected. That meant we had to hurry to get everything in place to trap him beforehand.

At the Costco, I tried a tracking spell on the front entrance. It was late and well after the store closed. No one should pay any attention to me. That didn't yield any leads, though. I tried several other potential locations before realizing I had to go back to the farm next to the big house where we'd battled the horde of zombies the necromancer had raised. I didn't think anyone would be stupid enough to go back to the original home after we flushed them out, but there might be a clue at the neighboring farm where the secret passage led about where they ran off to.

It was close to dawn by the time I neared the old farm. It was up ahead on the winding country road. I pulled into the driveway and got out of the Firebird to look around. My Fae night vision made the nearly moonless night bright as day. The barn and other outbuildings had fallen into disrepair over the years this farm had been abandoned. Everything looked the same way it had looked the night Chip and I were here a few weeks before. I stopped as I scanned the area again before going into the house. The undergrowth in front of the detached garage next to the house had been pressed flat. Someone had driven in or out of it recently.

I walked over to the side of the garage and peered in the window. Years of dust and filth clouded the glass, but I could see well enough in the early dawn sunlight to spot the late-model sedan parked inside. The red LED for the alarm system blinked in the center of the dashboard. The car hadn't been there when we'd come before. In fact, the garage door had been open when Chip and I were here the last time. Would the idiot be stupid enough to come back here and stay? Based on what I saw, and the debit card use nearby two days before, the answer was yes.

My hand dropped to my waist and rested on the hilt of my sword, clipped to my belt. It was time to flush this guy out from his hiding place. First, though, I had to make sure he didn't get away. I went back to the Firebird and started the engine. I pulled forward and then backed in so I was parked across the front of the garage entrance. If he managed to outrun me, he wouldn't be going anywhere.

With that escape option covered, all I had to do was find the guy. He had to be in the farmhouse or one of the other nearby buildings. Standing beside the Firebird, I looked around again, searching for any signs that might indicate where the necromancer might be hiding. The house was the obvious choice, but Chip and I had been through that before. Aside from rousting the zombie nest in the basement and sub-basement, there'd been no sign of a human living there.

I shifted my gaze to the barn and the attached milk shed. The large stainless-steel tank in the shed had been used to hold the fresh milk until it could be collected by truck. It had fallen into disuse, but there was a shiny, new deadbolt lock installed on the door into the shed. Why lock up a thousand-gallon steel tank and tubing?

That had to be where he was hiding, but it was equally likely he'd seen me drive in and was watching me now. I needed to come at the shed from another direction without being observed. I had to get him to think I was looking elsewhere. With the timetable pushed up by my aunt's sudden departure, I needed to catch this guy tonight. He couldn't get away again.

I drew my sword and entered the house instead. If I could get to the far side quickly, I could exit via a back window and circle around behind the house, the garage, and get around to the rear of the barn. I had to be quick and take advantage of the long shadows cast by the house and surrounding trees to cover my movements.

The kitchen door opened easily. It was unlocked. I rushed inside, ready for trouble. When I didn't see any of the undead, I turned right and ran through the house, sprinting through the rooms so fast, I should evade any zombies hiding in wait for me.

When I got to a formal living room with moldy furniture and fixtures, I approached the window against the back wall. The wooden frame looked warped and swollen from years of disuse. It took a minute to work the sash upward and make a gap big enough for me to slip through to the back yard. I lowered myself to the ground and crouched there next to the farmhouse while I prepared for the next part of my plan.

My hand came up to my necklace and the old silver charm hanging there. I closed my eyes and said the word of power that would shroud me in shadow. It was a spell that only worked at night. It would suffice to hide me as I worked my way around to the side and behind the garage.

I opened my eyes. A slight haze from the spell hovered at the edge of my vision like a layer of dark gauze wrapped around my face but leaving my eyes mostly free in the center. I ducked low and stuck to the shadowed outline of the house and a few big oak trees next to it.

At the corner, I snuck a peek around it to check the milk shed. I didn't detect any movement there. So far, so good. I crouched low and dashed across the open ground between the house and the garage. I dove into the shadows beside the building and started moving around the back to travel down the rear side and head for the barn next.

Once again, I looked around to see if there was any sign of the necromancer in the windows along the side of the milk shed. I didn't see anything. Deciding it was time to take a chance, I ran for the side of the barn and the partially open door there. Maybe I could avoid going all the way around the large building and cut through the center to get to the milk shed instead.

I caught myself barely in time to keep from plummeting through a gaping hole in the barn's wooden plank floor. I started to work my way around the opening in the floor, then stopped. If I could drop down inside, I might be able to gain access to the milk shed from a different level. That would give me a definite advantage.

The hole's jagged edges made it tricky finding a spot to safely climb down to the stone floor below. I found a spot on the far side where I could hang down and drop to the basement level. I landed in a crouch and scanned the near blackness around me. Even my Fae night vision had trouble piercing the dark corners of the large room.

The scrape of a boot froze me midway to standing. I wasn't alone. My hand dropped to the hilt of my sword a split second before ten shambling bodies rushed out of the shadows. I didn't get a chance to draw before the first of them were on me. The weight of their bodies crushed me back and down.

A yelp of panic escaped me and all I could think was the hope that someone would avenge my tragic death at the hands of these ravenous undead. At least Fae were mostly immune to becoming zombies themselves, so I could avoid that particular horror.

I waited for the biting and feeding to begin.

Nothing happened. They held me down and gripped my arms tightly enough so I couldn't move, but none of them bit me.

"Good. Good, my pets," a man's voice said from the darkness. "Now bring her along. I have much about which to ask our guest."

I struggled to lift my head and see who was talking. It had to be the necromancer, but I didn't know much about him. Neither Chip nor I had laid eyes on him the last time here. The good news was these zombies weren't going to eat me. The bad news was I hadn't told Warren or Chip exactly where I was going tonight. It was going to be a while before either of them came looking for me.

22

Chip

I woke up and checked my phone first thing to see if Rose had an update on locating a necromancer. The lack of a message from her overnight surprised me. Rose was never shy about texting me with new information at all hours of the day and night. I sent a message to her to fill me in on her progress and then got up to get Addy ready for school. It had been a late night again for him. He fought with me about going to bed, even after I'd had to punish him for taking his tomahawk to school. That kid needed to get up and go to school, even though he was tired. I needed him out of the house so I could connect with Rose about getting Sadie back.

Bernard waited for me in the kitchen. He sipped at a mug of black coffee and frowned when I walked in. "Any word on our girl?"

"No," I said. "I know she's alive and reasonably well. I can tell that much through our connection, but that's all. I don't suppose you have felt anything from her?"

"She's too far away from me to connect to her. I can't get any sleep during the daytime either. Her dreams help fuel my own dreams and sleep. That's all part of the relationship. I'm going to have to go and find another kid or see if Brunna will let me share with her when Addy sleeps."

"No sharing," Brunna declared. She shuffled into the kitchen in a stained white terrycloth bathrobe. "Addy's dreams are mine to deal with."

"Surely you can make an exception in Bernard's case, Brunna." I didn't want to lose Bernard from our family yet. Kids eventually outgrew their bed trolls and Sadie couldn't be far off from aging out of needing Bernard anymore. Still, I'd hoped she'd hold onto her little kid vibe a little bit longer.

"No," Brunna said. "Sadie's a growing girl and it's time Bernard moved on to find another child of Unusual parents who need a bed troll for their baby."

Bernard scowled, matching my expression. I could tell he didn't think it was time to make that change either.

"Hang in there a little longer, Bernard. Rose and I have a plan to get her back soon."

Bernard didn't seem convinced. He just nodded. "I hope so. I don't want to find a new home yet."

We let the conversation drop when Addy came in. He looked tired, but still had a bounce in his step. "Bernard, did you hear about my adventure at school?"

"It wasn't an adventure," I corrected. "You are not allowed to take weapons to school."

"I know that, now. When can I get it back? I have to practice throwing it in the back yard."

I scowled. "You're not getting the weapon back until we talk with Aunt Rose about it. She's your weapons master and I'm sure she'll want to talk with you about it during training."

Addy's shoulders sagged.

I pressed on with the day's agenda. "Right now, you need to get breakfast and then it'll be time to go and catch the bus."

"Awww, do I have to go to school? I thought I could stay home and help you find Sadie. I'm supposed to grow up to be her protector. How can I do that if I don't learn how?"

His argument surprised me. He'd never pressed on this aspect of his own destiny before. He must be missing his sister a lot for him to bring it up now.

"Eat your breakfast. There'll be time after school to help out if we need it. Right now, you have school to do."

"People are asking about where Sadie is." Addy said. "Do I keep telling them she's sick? I don't like lying to people. You and Aunt Rose always say that's wrong."

"We can't tell them the truth, buddy." I struggled to come up with an explanation that would help him justify his deception. "This is just like how you hide your Fae side from your human friends. They wouldn't understand that part of you, so you don't show it to them. It's the same thing. This is an Unusual problem and we have to handle it without people at school knowing."

That answer seemed to satisfy him for now. I switched on the TV on the wall over the counter so he could watch cartoons and eat his cereal and toaster pastry. It wasn't the best breakfast, but it would do for this morning. I had too much on my mind to deal with serving up a real breakfast with cut fruit and fresh-cooked eggs.

I ran upstairs while Brunna and Bernard were down in the kitchen with Addy and got dressed in jeans and a T-shirt. I pulled a sweatshirt over that and slipped on my sneakers. I got back downstairs in time to watch him finish up and put his dishes in the sink. I noticed the sink was full of dirty dishes and resolved to deal with that later, after I caught up with Rose.

Once Addy was dressed, we walked down to the bus stop and he got on without any further discussion about his sister. I wasn't off the hook, though. The nosy mom squad knew something was going on. Their radar for drama and community news was uncanny.

Barbara and Ellie hung back after the rest of the moms left and walked back to the cul-de-sac with me. Barb, the knockout blonde divorcee, was always the more inquisitive of the pair and she led off the questioning.

"I see Sadie's still under the weather. What's she got? Is it that flu bug that's going around? My Phoebe came down with it, but she was only home for a few days. Of course, she'd get to cheer practice from her deathbed if she had to, so I couldn't keep her home longer. The high school still needed a note from our doctor before she could come back."

"It's something like that. I've been in touch with our doctor. They'll take care of it."

Ellie, the rounder and shorter of the two neighbors, said, "I'd be worried Addy might get it, too. Or maybe you, Chip. You be careful you don't get it, too."

"I'm taking precautions, ladies. I appreciate the attention, but you both know me well enough by now. I've got this Mr. Mom thing down by now."

Ellie giggled. "Oh, Chip, we know that. We're just starved for information. We're the only other mostly at-home parents in this part of the neighborhood. We all have to stick together, don't we?"

"I suppose we do," I replied. "I'll let you know if I think Sadie's thing is spreading to Addy or me. I'm hoping she'll be back at school in a few days." I held up both hands. "Fingers crossed."

That brought smiles from both ladies. They were good friends and meant the best for the most part. Of course, I couldn't trust them with any of the supernatural problems we had. They were oblivious to it all and that was all good. I pictured their horrified reactions to learning about werewolves, vampires, and Fae all living in the community around them. It brought a smile to my face.

I waved as they kept walking down to their homes and turned in at my house. It was time to track down Rose and see what she'd been up to overnight. My phone still didn't have any messages and I decided to call her directly. The message picked up from her voicemail right away. That meant her phone was off, or she'd deliberately shunted me off to voicemail.

Bernard and Brunna had returned upstairs to their lairs under the beds by the time I went back inside the house. The uneasy feeling at the back of my mind when I thought about Rose wouldn't go away and I decided to call Warren to see if he'd heard from her. I didn't like to go around her to call him like that. Usually, she handled all the contacts with the werewolf when we needed his services.

He picked up on the third ring. "Hey, Chip. I'm surprised to hear from you. Did Rose ask you to call?"

"No, I was hoping you'd heard from her. She was looking into something regarding Sadie and Terrence last night and she hasn't checked in with me."

"Hmmm, that isn't like her. She hasn't reached out to me, either, if that's why you're calling."

"It is. I was hoping she was with you or told you where she was going. I think her phone's off so I don't think we can track her that way."

Warren laughed. "There are a lot of ways to track her, Chip. The phone is just one of them. I have another way, but you have to swear you won't tell her about it. It's super-secret and I don't want her getting pissed at me for it."

It was my turn to laugh. "What? You didn't have her chipped, did you?"

"Good gods, no. But she'll think it's just as bad. I put a tracker in her Firebird's engine."

I knew what he meant. "You're right. She'll think that's equally violating. That car's like a baby to her. Still, if she's in trouble and we can locate her, it'll be worth it."

Warren paused for a while, and I waited patiently. After ten long seconds, he nodded. "She's north of town, off in the countryside."

"Let me see."

"I'll send you the location."

A second later, my phone chirped. I opened the maps app and stared at the screen. It took me a second to orient myself to the map, then I understood. "That's the farm next to where we tracked that necromancer before. I'm sure she told you about the zombies we ran into."

"She did. She had me run down some information on the guy. I tracked his financials and figured out someone was using his debit card around town."

I snapped my fingers. "Rose must've looked at the farm for the guy. If she's still there, then she might have found him."

Warren grimaced. "I don't like second guessing her, but if she's still there after being out last night, then—"

"Then she's in trouble."

"You want to meet me there or have me swing by on my way to get you? I have to drive right past you." He huffed and puffed as he said it and I realized he was running.

"Pick me up. I'll be waiting out front."

Warren hung up and I ran to get my sword. The Guardian's weapon was magically collapsed to just a hilt. I clipped the small sheath to my belt at the small of my back and pulled on a jacket. I double checked to make sure the house was locked up and then went out through the garage to wait for Warren.

I was closing the garage door when the werewolf investigator pulled up in his SUV. I jumped in the passenger seat, and he pulled away while I still worked at buckling the seatbelt.

Warren pounded the steering wheel. "She should've had one of us go with her. I didn't realize she would go out on her own."

"Rose is a big girl," I said. I was reassuring myself as much as Warren. "There aren't many things she can't handle on her own out there. You and I are just window dressing compared to her when it comes to the fighting stuff."

"That doesn't mean she doesn't need backup sometimes." Warren stomped on the brakes to make the turn off the highway onto a back country road.

"Is this the best way there?"

He flashed his teeth in a fierce grin. "It's a back way. We'll come up on the other side of the farm property. There will be a tractor road connecting the fields we can use to get there faster."

I caught the feral glint in his now-glowing yellow eyes. I'd never been this close to a werewolf on the verge of shifting before. It was terrifying. I worked to ignore the low growls coming from the seat beside me and focused on the winding road ahead. I hoped his inner wolf didn't take over before the SUV stopped moving.

Warren spun the wheel and swerved onto a dirt and gravel lane between two fields filled with the stubble of harvested corn stalks dotting them. I was glad he slowed down, but only a little. He was still going way too fast for the quality of road. SUV or not, this modern road vehicle wasn't built for this kind of punishment. Neither were my nerves.

"We need to get there in one piece, buddy. I can't regenerate the way you can if you roll this thing or smack into a tree."

I turned to look out the front and my eyes went wide. The farm lane ended in a row of trees fifty yards ahead.

Warren slammed on the brakes.

The SUV fishtailed as it threatened to spin around and roll over. Warren struggled with control of the wheel, and I worried he was going to crash us both into the rapidly approaching line of trees.

We slid to a stop a bare two feet from a pair of tall ash trunks covered in twisted vines.

"Dammit, Warren. I thought you said this lane would lead to the farm?"

"It does," he growled. He extended a taloned finger straight ahead past the trees. Then he jumped out, leaving the door open as he sped off between the trees for the distant farmhouse visible across the large field on the far side of the tree line.

At first, I thought about taking the SUV and driving back down the lane to get there by road. I realized Warren was right. This was the quickest way, as much as I didn't like the thought of running across the field for a few hundred yards to get to the farm.

Warren was a snarling, two-legged half-man wolf now. He'd left a trail of shredded clothing dotting the field behind him.

I ran after him, trying to pick my way with care so I didn't snap an ankle in a groundhog hole because I wasn't paying attention. There was no way I'd catch up with the enraged werewolf, but I held my own.

By the time I jogged into the farmyard between the house and the outbuildings, Warren was nowhere in sight.

I struggled to catch my breath as I walked around the garage. "Warren! Where the hell are you?"

"He-e-e-errrre." His snarling voice carried across to me from nearby. I rounded the corner and spotted Rose's Firebird pulled up there. Warren had pulled open the door and was half inside it rummaging around for something.

He popped back out from inside, his massive wolf muscles rippling beneath his fur. He rested his clawed hands on the roof of the sports car and glared at me. I was glad he was on my side.

I summoned up enough bravery to ask, "What did you find?"

"It'ssss what I didn't find," he said. "Herrrr sword is missing."

I looked around the farmyard. Nothing moved anywhere I looked in the bright sunlight of the brisk autumn morning. "So where is she? Can you smell her out or something?"

Warren sniffed at the air for a few seconds and shrugged, shaking his head at the same time. Then a light breeze blew in, shifting the direction of the airflow, and Warren's glowing yellow eyes widened. He pointed in the direction of the old red wooden barn. "Therrrrre."

I reached back for my sword's hilt while I ran towards the barn. I concentrated on the weapon in my hand and touched my inner mana. A second later, the blade snapped out from the hilt as the magical energy fed the hidden blade's mechanism. A yard of sharpened silver-steel alloy extended out from my hand, leading the way as I charged into the barn.

My feet skidded to a stop just in time to stop me from tumbling into a gaping hole in the wooden plank floor. Warren ran up beside me, sniffed around, growled once, and leaped down into the darkness inside the opening.

"I guess we're going down there." I peered into the darkness and then remembered to access my Guardian sight from within my shark's tooth charm around my neck. Once I could see better, I collapsed the blade and clipped the hilt onto my belt. I looked until I found a place I could hang down to drop to the floor below.

Warren waited for me to join him and take the lead. There was only one clear exit from the large stone room. I used my slightly enhanced dark vision and walked to the open door that led onto a stone-lined passage.

I walked down a narrow underground hallway to a closed door ahead with light shining beneath it. After drawing my sword again, I placed my free hand on the doorknob and twisted it. Bright light splashed out, lighting the passage as the door swung inward.

Rose said, "About time you got here, Chip."

23

Rose

I stopped fighting against the animated corpses as soon as I realized the zombies weren't trying to hurt me, just restrain me. That was odd and worth pausing to understand. The zombies we'd encountered before here at the farm had been the mindless, brain-eating kind. These might be more like the few sentient zombies I'd gotten to know over the years who were mostly like regular folks, if you could ignore the random body parts falling off them from time to time.

The man who'd spoken out of the darkness hadn't said anything else and the zombies were silent, too. If they could speak, they weren't the talkative kind. I let them press in around me and shuffle me in the center of their rotting horde towards the door at the far side of the large stone room in the barn's basement.

When they reached the door, they parted and left an opening through which I could walk. I resisted reaching out with my sword arm to start hacking at the undead around me. They weren't attacking me and if they started, there would only be one outcome with them pressed in around me in this confined space.

I tried the rusty doorknob with my free hand. It twisted and the latch released. I pushed the door open to reveal a narrow stone passageway leading to another door. Light shined beneath this one. I walked to it and took a breath. I didn't have to look behind me. I heard the shuffling feet of the zombies who'd filled the hallway behind me. There was no going back. It was forward or nothing. Besides, it was time to meet the guy who was the reason for my visit.

I opened the door and the bright, yellow light of a single incandescent bulb hanging from the beams of the ceiling filled the room. A small, rusty bed frame sat against one wall with a musty mattress on it. A rolled sleeping bag and a pillow lay atop the mattress. A small table and a single chair were the only other furniture in the room.

The thing that drew my instant attention was the person standing in the center of the room. It was a middle-aged man of maybe forty-five, judging from the graying temples. He wore simple blue jeans and a red flannel shirt. He could have passed as a simple farmer in a crowd except for the dark energy I sensed pulsing from within him.

"You're the evil necromancer we tracked here."

"You're the fairy girl who's been trying to kill me."

His description irked me. "I'm not a fairy. I'm Fae. There's a difference."

"I'm not evil. I'm practical. There's a difference."

I wasn't in a position to argue semantics with the guy, so I just nodded. After an awkward pause where neither of us spoke, I turned to close the door and shut the zombies in the passage behind me.

"Don't do that. They don't like being separated from me if they think I'm in danger."

"What makes you think you're in danger? You have all the power here."

He smiled and pointed at my sword, hanging down from my hand at my side. "The second you shut that door, it'll just be you and me in here alone. I suspect you could kill me with a single swipe of that blade. It looks sharp."

"It is." I took pride in my tools. "It seems we're at a bit of a stand-off. What do you suggest we do now? You sounded like you wanted to talk when you told your friends to bring me to you."

"I do. My name is Scott. Scott Wains. I'm the farmer who used to work this land."

"I'm Rose Eldersdottir. I'm the person making sure a zombie horde doesn't take over the area and hurt the people I love." I looked back over my shoulder at the zombies behind me. Having them there itched at that spot between my shoulder blades.

"I'll tell you what, Rose. I'll have my friends pass through into the basement of the milk shed. That way they won't be behind you. In exchange, you set your blade down on that table and grab the chair. We'll both sit down over here by the cot and have a little heart to heart."

I wasn't in a position to argue. I could probably kill him like he said. But that would surely release the zombies to attack, and I'd never fight my way out of here alone. I needed to bide my time. Besides, I needed this guy, as much as it irked me to ask him for help. Sadie was my number one priority.

"That sounds reasonable. I'll go over to the table, and you move the undead to the next room."

Scott nodded. He pointed to an open door behind him. "In there, my pets. I'm in no danger with this woman. Go and rest yourselves. I'll be in to tend to you soon."

The shuffling horde at my back passed behind me and through the doorway into a darkened space next door. Ignoring the raised hairs and shivers running up my back to my neck, I kept my back to them and walked over to the table in the corner. I set my sword down on it.

When the final zombie passed from the room, I picked up the small, wooden chair and carried it over to set it next to the bed. Scott came over and sat down at the end of the thin mattress.

I sat down opposite him. "You can't like living down here. Why don't you live in the farmhouse?"

He shook his head and his eyes turned sad. "Too many happy memories there to bear. I'd see my wife at every turn, in each room."

Realization of what he meant dawned on me. "How long has she been gone?"

"Just under a year," he replied.

I was starting to see what might be going on here. "You're very powerful for just a year of practice. I heard of those who practice necromancy for years and who have trouble raising and controlling a single zombie. You've got at least two dozen you've raised."

"It's a matter of power and focus. Before my Darcy passed, I was a prosperous farmer. The only thing I used my considerable magical ability for was to ensure my crops grew tall and strong. It never occurred to me to use my power for anything other than giving life to the seeds I grew. We lived a good life for many years until the cancer took her from me."

I understood the pain of loss in his voice at least in part. I might have been tempted to do something drastic to bring back Lili after her accident, if there had been more than ashes left of her. I nodded back at the open door where the zombies had gone. "Is she one of them?"

"No, I haven't perfected my technique yet. She'd be angry with me if I brought her back as a withered shell of herself like she was at the end. They are people I've—" He stopped himself for a second before he opened his mouth to continue.

"They're the dead you've practiced on, right?" I said, interrupting him.

He nodded. "It's horrible, I know, but I've learned how to keep them from attacking people on sight. They're docile now, almost whole-minded people again."

Horrible didn't begin to describe how I felt inside. My guts twisted with disgust at the way this man had used his grief to justify his actions. I took back my earlier thoughts that I might have done the same. But I could see he wasn't inherently evil. He'd done evil things, but he had a core that might be redeemable. And I needed to find it and turn it to our side. The Seer had alluded to the fact we'd need a necromancer. This guy was our best chance of getting Sadie back unhurt.

"Scott, my family needs someone with your skills. A child has been kidnapped. She was taken by a person who was brought forward from the past. He was killed in his own time, but somehow powerful magic reanimated him and did so in a way that brought him all the way back. He looks as alive as you and me."

A glimmer of hope brightened Scott's eyes. "That is what I'm trying to do for Darcy. How did they accomplish this?"

"We don't know. But perhaps if you help us, you'll be able to see how it could be done."

Scott didn't hesitate at all. "I'll do whatever you want me to do. Just tell me and I'll do it."

"That's just it, Scott. I don't know what it is you're to do for us. I only know it has to do with necromancy, and that without it, we cannot defeat this person. Will you help us, even if it doesn't help you recover your wife?"

"I must know how he did this. I will help you. There will be clues to how it was done and that is enough to convince me." Scott leaned forward and extended his hand. "You have a deal, Rose Eldersdottir."

I shook his hand, ignoring the revulsion inside and the sense that I'd just entered a pact with a kind of serial killer.

Scott stood. "Let me go and get us something to eat. We must seal our agreement with a meal. It's the only way. I'll be right back."

I waited while he left me alone in the room. I considered leaving. The way back to the barn was clear and I could figure out a way to climb back up to the main floor. But if I left, then the deal I'd just made could fall apart. As icky as I felt about it, we needed Scott and his skills. I only hoped they'd be enough to accomplish what would need to be done when the time came. I had a feeling that there was more to this than just casting a spell.

While I waited, I checked my phone for messages. The stone of the barn's foundation must have a lot of iron in it. I had zero signal down here. Instead, I settled for playing a matching jewel game on the device and bided my time.

More than an hour later, Scott returned with a broad tray of food. He smiled at me as he entered. "I wasn't sure you'd be here with I came back."

"I was serious. You and I need each other. I don't enter into deals like this one lightly."

He set the tray down on the bed close to my chair. The tray had more food than I'd expected when he left. There was a platter piled high with fresh pancakes, bacon, country ham, and sausages. A serving bowl next to the platter held a heaping portion of steaming scrambled eggs. There was a pot of coffee and two mugs, too.

He noticed my reaction to the spread on the tray. "Sorry, Rose. It's a typical farmer's breakfast and old habits die hard. Besides, I didn't know what you'd like, so I sort of made everything."

"It's quite the spread, but I think I can find something to eat here." I put on a smile and picked up one of the plain white china plates. I served myself a pair of pancakes and two slices of crispy bacon. A small, white pitcher had what smelled like real maple syrup in it. Then I poured some over the pancakes and even a little on the bacon.

When I finished, I sat back after selecting a knife and fork from the tray beside the platter "This looks delicious. Thank you."

We ate in silence, which I appreciated. I'd gotten what I came here to get. My mind had already shifted to the next part of the problem. How to lure Terrence out of hiding with Sadie so we could set the trap for him. We had a limited time to figure out that part.

A female zombie shuffled in. She didn't look like she'd been dead that long and I spotted the scars of track marks up and down her arm from long drug use. It seemed that Scott had used the corpses of unclaimed vagrants and Jane Does to practice his infernal arts.

The zombie groaned something unintelligible to Scott. He nodded and waved for the girl to leave. He turned to me and said, "There are two men here. At least I think that's what she said. It's hard to understand her with a half-rotted tongue. It sounded like she said something about a hairy one."

I nodded in reply. "My guess is they're both here for me. One is a werewolf friend of mine. That would make the other one Chip. Maybe we should go out to meet them?"

Scott paused and looked off in the distance as if he were staring through another's eyes. "No need. They're coming this way. I think they'll be here shortly."

"Then we have time to finish this fine meal." I took my time and took the final few bites of bacon from what I had taken. "This was very good. Thank you."

"I haven't forgotten how to be a good host."

I ignored the fact that he'd used his zombies to try and kill us a few weeks before. We needed each other. I would have to overlook the previous interactions, for now.

The door to the passage back to the barn opened. Chip stood there, sword in his hand, ready to go. A hulking hairy form stood in the hallway's shadows behind him.

"About time you got here, Chip," I said. I nodded at the man in jeans and a red flannel shirt standing beside me. "This is Scott. He's going to help us. We need to get started planning how we're going to trap Terrence."

24

Chip

The next twenty-four hours flew by as Rose, Warren, Scott, and I worked at putting the plan into motion. With Aunt Allura, Reston, and the cook gone, it was easy for Rose to give the groomsman who lived in an apartment over the barn the weekend off. With that done, Rose and Warren started their preparations for what was coming next. I excused myself from the final preparations as I needed to run get Addy off the bus. I wanted to get him settled with Ellie and her kids. That was an integral part of the plan. Ellie was expecting Addy to come over and spend the night starting at dinnertime. I had just enough time to get his homework finished before we had to leave to go over to the neighbor's house.

"Addy, you're all finished. Put your schoolwork away while I go and get your overnight bag together. Miss Ellie is expecting you for dinner."

"I hope it's not something gross."

"That's enough of that, Addison Proctor. You'll be nice and eat some of whatever she makes for you. She's helping us bring Sadie home. She thinks we're taking her to an overnight medical test at the hospital. You have to do your part to help us keep the secret about your sister." The doorbell rang and I jumped up, wondering if Ellie had decided to come over and fetch Addy for me.

I ran to the front door. I didn't want to keep the jolly neighbor waiting. My hand pulled the door open as soon as I got there, and I put a smile on my face to greet Ellie.

"Chip," Patty Peyton said. "I stopped by to drop off Sadie's homework. I had Astrid pick it up to bring over."

"Oh, uh, yeah. Thanks!" I reached for the canvas tote bag she held. "Is that the homework?"

"Yes. Can I come in? She's not still contagious, is she? I asked Astrid, but she didn't seem to know what illness it was that had Sadie sidelined."

I glanced back over my shoulder, my mind swirling with possible answers that would get rid of Patty before I had to leave with Addy.

"Um, now's not a really good time, Patty. I'm just about to get dinner together."

"Let me help. You must have your hands full with taking care of Sadie if she's that sick." She pushed her way past me. "Besides, my social calendar is suddenly clear, and I thought maybe I could come give you a hand."

I knew what that meant. Her latest boyfriend had left her, and she was trolling for some companionship.

Patty and I had developed to become a sort of friends with benefits thing where she dropped in whenever she was between her searches for a steady man in her life. I didn't mind usually, but tonight was definitely bad timing.

"Patty, with Sadie sick, it's really not a good time. Maybe we can get together this weekend?"

"My ex has the kids tonight, Chip. I'm in one of those moods." She rubbed up against me and purred in my ear. "You like it when I'm feeling this way."

I peeled myself away from Patty. I needed a way to get rid of her and quickly. I needed to get moving and meet Rose. I didn't have time for even a quickie with Patty. Only one thing would stop her.

"Rose is coming over, Patty. We've started seeing each other."

That stopped her prowling. She stood ramrod straight and stared at me. "You and Rose?"

Her eyes bored into mine, searching for something that would contradict what I'd just said.

"It's new and we're trying things out slowly for the kids." I kept my voice steady and even. I couldn't afford for her to see through my lies. "They need stability from the two of us. You understand, don't you? I can't have other women dropping over unannounced right now."

"You and Rose?" She repeated the words like she was trying them on for size.

"Yes." I moved back to the front door and held it open. "You have to go, Patty. I need you to leave now."

With her back stiff as a board and her head held high, Patty strode past me, turning sideways to fit through the gap between me and the open door. Her breast brushed against my arm as she passed. I knew she'd done that on purpose. She knew how much I had enjoyed them in the past. I got the sense from the cold smile on her face that she was telling me I wouldn't be enjoying them again any time soon.

"I left the tote bag with the homework on the sofa. Don't bother to return it." She walked off without another word and I shut the door. I hoped that encounter didn't indicate what the rest of the evening was going to be like.

I hadn't taken five steps away from the door when the bell rang again. I spun around and yanked it open. "Patty," I meant what I said. This can't work out. Not tonight."

"Excuse me, Chip?" Ellie said.

"Oh, my God. Excuse me. I didn't mean you, of course."

"I saw Patty walking away." The sly neighbor winked at me and walked into the entry hall. "I assume this means she's between men again?"

"Yes, I think so."

"Well," Ellie said as she passed into the family room. "If you ask me, that woman has always been trouble. She never seemed to know how to make do with what life gave her and always wants what others have. You should find someone else, someone who shares a common bond with the children."

I knew where she was going with this. She always had a twinkle in her eye when she saw me and Rose together.

"Sorry to say that ship has sailed, Ellie. Rose and I are not meant for each other."

"Sometimes what is obvious to others isn't to you. Time will tell, I suppose." She shifted gears. "Has Addy finished his homework?"

"We finished up right before you got here. All you have to do is feed him and get him in bed. Thank you for being willing to take him. I have to get to the hospital. Sadie rode over there with her Aunt Rose earlier."

"I hope the little dear feels better soon. It's a shame she got so ill."

"I know." I called up the stairs. "Addy, Miss Ellie is here. It's time to leave."

Addy bounced down the stairs with his soccer backpack over both shoulders. I'd packed it for him with his pajamas, a change for tomorrow, and his toothbrush. Ellie would take care of everything else.

As he passed by me, he leaned in and whispered, "Get Sadie back, Uncle Chip. I miss her."

"Me, too," I said. I waved bye to him and Ellie and watched them walk back across the street. Then I locked up the house and left. As I'd done so often since Sadie went missing, I reached out for her. I noticed the difference in the connection right away. She felt closer somehow. I still couldn't narrow down her direction like I used to, but she had moved from where they'd been keeping her. I was sure of it.

I pulled out my phone as I climbed into the minivan. Rose picked up as soon as the call went through.

"I hope you're on the way. There's a lot we have to do to prepare for Terrence coming for the lance. Tonight is the new moon."

"I think they might be on the way now. I can't be sure, but I think Sadie is on the move. She feels closer than before."

Rose cut loose with a string of curses and for a second, I thought she'd dropped the phone. Then she came back on. "Get over here, now. Pick up Scott on your way. Warren's still out rounding up a few friends to help keep the Dark Travelers busy."

"On it," I said. "I'll be there in thirty minutes. Traffic around town this time of day is insane."

"Make it sooner. It'll be dark soon and I worry that might be what Terrence is waiting for. He and the gang will hit the manor tonight for sure. They can't risk Aunt Allura coming back. She's very powerful and would be a formidable opponent." She hung up and I gunned the engine as I raced out of the development. My stomach was tied in knots. We had our chance to rescue Sadie tonight, but it was going to be dangerous, and I was sure Terrence wouldn't just let us have her in exchange for the Lance. He had to have something else planned with the arcane artifact and Gareth.

I wove in and out of traffic, trying my best to get there on time. The sun set behind me as I drove, and I hoped I'd make it before Terrence and his thugs. I couldn't let Rose take them on alone.

25

Rose

I hung up on Chip and looked around at the preparations I'd made at the front door of the home. I felt a little like the Home Alone kid with all the rapidly assembled defenses arrayed throughout the first floor. Hopefully, though, Terrence and the biker gang would take the bait and come right at the manor house. I wanted to inflict the maximum amount of damage when they tried to get inside.

The sun had already set low to the west. The light dimmed by the minute, and I knew I had little time left. I wondered where Warren was. He was supposed to be on his way back with a few members of his pack who owed me favors for some odd magical jobs I'd done for them over the years. If there was ever a time to call in markers from them, it was now. This fight had the potential to get ugly in a hurry.

My sensitive ears picked up a vehicle coming down the gravel lane to the house. At first, I thought it was Warren coming back. Then I looked for his SUV and realized I was wrong. The large black panel van had its lights off and drove too fast for its size and the narrowness of the tree-lined drive. The top of the van struck more than a few low-hanging branches as it barreled along.

Shit, I wasn't ready yet. Not that it mattered. Terrence had come and it was time to tango. I'd have to do what I could to bide my time while I waited for Chip and Warren to come and lend a hand.

I ran up the front steps to the door and darted inside, slamming it shut behind me. I had all the lights shut off. I could see fine, but the gang members were human spell casters. They'd have a hard time without lights. That wouldn't stop Terrence. He was Fae like me. But the rest of them would struggle.

I drew upon my mana and cast a quick and useful cant on the door. Then I picked up a crossbow propped beside the door and ran into the front parlor. I crouched by the open window and leveled the bow on the ledge there, waiting for an open shot.

The van pulled up to stop beside my Firebird. The back doors opened and at least a dozen shadowy figures hopped down to the driveway. Then Terrence climbed out of the cab's passenger side. He reached inside and pulled a bound Sadie out to stand her beside him. Her hands were tied in front of her, and her eyes were covered with a plain white blindfold.

"Search the house. This is the woman's car. She's here somewhere. I'll reward the one of you who finds her and brings her to me."

Five of the Dark Travelers ran towards the front door. I couldn't shoot Terrence, as much as I wanted to. I might hit Sadie. Instead, I aimed and let fly with the crossbow at the closer targets.

The first of the Travelers running up the walk went down, spinning around to the ground with a crossbow bolt jutting from his shoulder.

The others scattered, crouching and looking around for the source of the shot.

I braced the bow on the floor with my foot and reached down to draw the cable back and cock the bow for another shot.

"Get up, you idiots," Terrence shouted. "She's inside the house. The only way to get her is to rush in there. She can't shoot all of you."

The other Travelers by the rear of the van split up and ran around the sides of the manor and out of sight. The four unwounded ones crouching out front slowly rose when another shot didn't come right away.

At Terrence's continued urging they once again reached the front steps and started up. I raised the crossbow again and let loose with shot number two.

The nearest of the gang members screamed and dropped to the ground clutching the shaft jutting out from his hip. He'd probably never walk right on that side again. Not that I cared.

This time, instead of scattering, the other three ran the final few yards to the front door.

The first to reach the entrance screamed and fell backward waving his hands and clapping them together to try and put out the magical fire that had shot out from the door when he touched the knob. The final two Travelers ran down the stairs away from their burning comrade as the flames spread up his arms to his torso.

I quickly re-cocked the bow and ran for the back door. The others would be trying the kitchen entrance by now and I had a surprise waiting for them there as well. I needed to slow them down and make them think twice about entering. Hopefully the remaining two out front wouldn't realize the fire spell was a one-time deal.

A small explosion out back told me someone had triggered the spell I'd placed on the doormat outside the kitchen. I ran to the kitchen just as a second Dark Traveler tried the knob and pushed open the door.

I fired the crossbow from the hip as I ran in. The bolt took him in the chest and knocked him back into the one standing behind him. They both fell back into the yard behind the house. The one who'd stepped on the mat lay writhing on the grass. One leg was missing below the knee, with nothing but a smoldering stump to show for his going first.

There was no time to reload. I dropped the crossbow and reached back to draw my sword. I screamed my war cry and charged to block the door. I lunged in under the sword wielded by the next of the Travelers to try and enter.

He grunted in surprise when my blade slid through his heart and out the back of his leather jacket. His legs buckled and he twisted as he fell backward, dragging my sword along with him.

I tugged at the hilt to dislodge the blade for a second too long. One of the Travelers near the rear door pointed a leather gloved finger at me. A lance of foul green light shot from his hand.

The magical energy struck me in the chest and sent me flying back into the kitchen. I coughed and tried to breathe. The force of the blow had knocked the wind from me. The magic had burned a hole through my leather jacket, but my protective amulet had warded off most the fell energy directed at me.

Of course, that was enough for them to get inside. The Travelers in the back charged into the kitchen.

I stood, wavering a little as I gasped to draw breath. I reached back and pulled my silver tanto blade from my belt.

One of the gang crowding around me reached for my arm.

I slashed out and the razor-sharp blade cut deep into his forearm. I followed the attack with a spinning kick that caught the one sneaking up behind me unawares.

He took the full force of my booted heal on his square jaw. I felt the bone crack as his head whipped around. He went down and didn't get back up. He'd be drinking from a straw for a few months while that healed.

I jumped up from my fighting crouch and rolled on my back across the island countertop. Plates and a few utensils left there scattered as I swung around to land on my feet on the opposite side.

This maneuver avoided the other two closing in on me but also put me back close to the door.

Terrence shouted from inside the front of the house. "Take her alive. We need her power to supplement the girl's."

The grimaces on the faces around me told me they didn't like the command. Taking me alive meant they were going to get hurt doing it. I wasn't about to go down without a fight.

There were four of them in the kitchen now. Two reached for me across the counter while the other two circled around to take me from either side.

I slashed again with my knife but didn't connect. It did make the two across the island pull back, but my attack also opened me up to the two coming around to get in close.

I had a choice to make. I could only face one at a time. I turned my back on the shorter of the two and faced the bigger one advancing from my right.

He had two silver teeth glinting in the darkness as he snarled at me. He didn't charge, though. Instead, he extended both hands and clenched his fists.

I realized my error as an invisible force pounded down on my shoulders from his magical blow. It forced me down to my knees.

The one coming up behind me wrapped his arms around me, pinning my arms to my sides. I tried to reach up and cut at his gloved hands with my knife but a black leather boot from in front of me came down and struck my hand, knocking the blade away to spin across the floor.

I struggled to push back with my feet and topple the one holding me from behind, but I never got the chance. The one who'd climbed over the island to kick at my knife hand leaned down and punched me three times in rapid succession with powerful fists.

I started to black out on the second blow and barely felt the third. Darkness closed around me. My fight to defend the house was over.

26

Chip

I pushed the minivan to its limits, racing to get to Allura's farm. I called Scott and told him to meet me there. It would be faster than detouring to pick him up. I could sense Sadie well enough as I got closer to know she was somewhere ahead of me now. That could only mean that Terrence was ahead of me, too, and Rose faced them alone.

When I got to the turnoff to go down the lane to the manor house, I stopped. If I raced in there, they'd see me coming long before I could get there. Instead, I pulled to the side of the road beside the whitewashed post-and-board fence. I got out and locked the van, pulled out my sword and extended the blade from the hilt.

I was about to climb through the fence and start across the field towards the house when Warren pulled up in his SUV and parked behind the minivan. He got out along with two others, one man and one woman.

"You were going in there alone?" he asked.

"Sadie and Rose are in there."

"You sure?"

I nodded. "Sadie's close, I can sense that much, and Rose was on the phone with me right before I left to come here. Terrence must have gotten there ahead of us."

Warren nodded. "Good idea parking out here, then. Go on. We'll be along in a second."

I wasn't sure what he was waiting for, then I noticed his companions stripping off their clothes and piling them atop the hood of the SUV. They were getting ready to shift into werewolf mode.

They'd catch up to me soon enough once they changed. I climbed through the horizontal gap between two boards in the fence and ran across the grassy field. I startled a horse in the darkness. It whinnied and galloped off as I ran by. Other than that, I didn't see anything or anyone else all the way to the house.

Three racing wolf forms ran past me as I reached the circular driveway in front of the manor house. A big black panel van had parked beside Rose's car. There was no sign of anyone outside that I could see.

Warren and the others crouched beside me. It made me uneasy to be so close to so much lethal power. I reminded myself they were on my side.

"I smell burrrrnt flesh," the female werewolf said in a low snarl.

"Yessss, and blood, too," the one I thought was Warren said. In their naked humanoid wolf forms, it was hard to tell which of the two males was which.

"Where?" I asked.

The female pointed to the front door. I peered through the darkness and then realized I hadn't activated my Guardian charm's dark sight. As soon as I remedied that, I saw a charred body crumpled beside the open front door.

Warren said, "Check the back. I'll go in the front with Chip."

The other two wolf forms darted off in opposite directions around the house without saying a word.

I nodded and crouched low as I ran for the front door. Warren ran past me and leaped forward with a snarl. He landed atop a burly man lying on the ground. He had a crossbow through his hip.

The guy cried out in pain and fear.

"Don't kill him," I hissed in the suddenly broken silence. "He might know where everyone is."

Warren growled but pressed down on the fallen guy's chest while holding a taloned finger up to his lips to shush the now-crying gang member. The man's whimpers lowered to soft whines.

I continued past them and reached the front porch. A body lay off to the side. A crossbow bolt jutted out from the chest near the left shoulder. He appeared to be dead. So was the mostly charred corpse lying on the steps.

Kneeling there and trying to ignore the horrible stench of burned flesh and hair beside me, I leaned forward and tried to listen for any sounds coming from the house. I peered into the darkened entry hall but didn't see any movement. I didn't hear anything either.

"Wait here," I told Warren. I was being way braver than I probably should have been. It would've been smarter to let the werewolf go in first while I waited with the injured enemy. But Sadie was in there somewhere and that overrode my judgement. I had to get to her.

I darted the rest of the way up the steps and ran inside, leading with my gleaming sword. When I encountered no one in the rooms at the front of the house, I started down the hallway to the rear. I passed the formal dining room and what passed for a study without encountering anyone. I reached the door to the kitchen and stopped. A shadow on the kitchen floor moved right before I entered.

I was about to leap into the room and engage with the other person when a growling voice said, "It is I, Guarrrrdian."

Realizing it was the female werewolf, I relaxed a little. "I'm coming in."

I walked into the kitchen. The door to the back yard was open. A body lay outside, missing a leg. Another was right beside the door with a crossbow bolt's fins sticking out from a bloody hole in the stomach. Rose had taken a bunch of them down with her. The question was where was she and how many were left?

"Anyone else out back?" I asked the female wolf.

"No. I sssent Leon to check the barrrrns and carrrrrriage house. Therrre is no one herrre but the dead."

"Wait here and keep your ears and nose open. They have to be somewhere close by. I can sense Sadie is very near." I checked the other rooms at the back of the house and then went up the winding back stairs to the second floor. A quick pass through there revealed no one else inside the house.

One thing I noticed was a definite tug of my sense of Sadie. It was pulling me back to the first floor as if she was somewhere below me. I went down the front hallway steps and then ran around to the basement door to reach the stairs that ran beneath them. The lights were on in the basement, and I took my time going down to avoid creaking the old steps.

The old unfinished basement had a dirt floor and was lined with the stone walls of the original manor foundation. Old wooden shelves lined a few of the walls with rows of preserves and pickles from Ms. McGarry's hard work running the kitchen. Other than that, and the old furnace, there was not a sign of anyone down here.

After searching for several minutes, I couldn't stop the sense that Sadie was close to me and somehow still below me, but there was not a door or other stairs going down from there. I knew that meant there was a secret entrance, but I soon gave up the search. I hoped I'd be able to get an answer from the lone survivor of the attack on the house.

I returned to the first floor. The werewolf named Leon had returned from his search of the barns and outbuildings. He and the female whose name I still didn't know stood at the front door waiting for me as I came back from my search of the basement. I walked past them and out onto the porch.

"Bring him to me," I said to Warren.

I waited until Warren dragged the whimpering man up to where I stood. "Where are they?"

"I-I-I don't know. They all went inside with the Master and didn't come back out."

I reached down and gripped the stub of the crossbow bolt in the guy's hip. With a twist of my wrist, I pushed forward, pressing the bolt deeper into the wound.

He howled in pain. "Stop, please. I swear that's all I know. The Master said the way was clear. Then, he took the girl and the witch hunter inside through the front door. I haven't seen anyone else until you all got here. Please, do something about the pain."

I glanced at Warren and nodded. He balled up his clawed hand into a fist and punched the guy in the head. He fell back unconscious.

My guts twisted in a knot. "They've got to be inside there somewhere, but I don't know how to get to the vault. Did Rose tell you anything about how to access it?"

"Rose? Do you think she'd share how to access the royal family's secret vault?"

"Yeah, I guess you're right, but there has to be a way to find out." I ran through my options and decided I had no choice. I had to contact Reston, the butler. He'd know how to get into the vault if anyone other than Allura did.

It took me several long, agonizing seconds to find his number. I'd been given it once in a text message by Rose to make an appointment to bring the kids over to see their great-aunt. I composed what I was going to say in my head and then tapped to place the call.

Reston picked up right away, catching me by surprise. He was supposed to be on vacation with the mistress away.

"Master Proctor, may I presume you're calling with regard to some problem at the mistress' manor?"

My jaw dropped. "How did you know?"

"It's my job to know everything about the mistress and her home. What has happened? I got a notification that someone had tripped the silent alarm entering the vault."

"There's an alarm? Great, so the police are coming?" I knew Rose didn't want to involve them, but at this point, I was willing to accept any help I could get.

"Of course not. However, I am on my way. I'll be there in ten minutes."

"There's not enough time to wait for you. They have Sadie and Rose down there. I need to get to them. Tell me how to get inside. Is there a way we can get in and sneak up on them?"

For the first time in the call, Reston was silent. He stopped talking for so long that I worried the call had disconnected.

"Master Proctor, what I am about to tell you is a secret reserved only for the most loyal members of the family and retainers. It is not to be shared with anyone. Do you understand?"

I glanced around at the three werewolves standing beside me and shrugged. "Sure. I won't tell anyone."

The butler went silent again before saying, "There is another entrance besides the entrance in the basement. Between the house and the old stone barn is a springhouse. Inside, you'll find a triangular stone at the back wall. Press it while you say the words, 'the Queen awaits.' That will open an alternative method to access the vault. Whoever has taken Miss Rose and the young princess will be watching the main entrance from the basement. They won't know about this alternate entrance. That will bring you in behind them."

"You're the best, Reston."

"I'll be there soon. I would still advise you to wait for me."

"I can't. There's no time. I know something bad is happening down there. I have to go. Come find us when you get here." I disconnected the call and waved to Warren.

He pointed at the lights of another vehicle coming down the lane. As it got closer, I made out the shape of an old farm pickup truck. Scott was finally here. The farmer climbed out of his truck and sauntered up to where the four of us stood by the manor's entrance.

"I see the action has started already. Do you still need my help?"

"Yes," I replied. "Very much. We're about to go and confront them down beneath the farm. Follow me. We have a back way in."

Warren jogged next to me as we rounded the side of the house. "I could hearrrr you. Rrrrreston told you not to sharrre this. Now Scott will know too."

"The butler will get over it. Besides, if any of you share this, you know what Rose will do to you." I glanced back at the two werewolves and the necromancer trailing behind us. They all nodded.

We reached the old springhouse. It had a fieldstone foundation with a small, pitched wooden roof covered in shingles. Narrow stone steps led down into the partially sunken floor where the natural spring bubbled up to form a pool contained by a low masonry wall.

I ignored the cool chill created by the flowing water and walked to the far wall built up against a small hill next to the spring. I used my dark sight to see, but even with that it was difficult to make out the shapes of the individual stones set in the wall. With my phone in hand,

I turned on the flashlight function and shined it. The smooth triangular stone stood out among the rough surface of the irregular stones around it.

"Here we go," I said. I pressed at the stone with the palm of my hand. "The Queen awaits." The stone sunk into the wall about an inch, and something clicked. A section of the wall swung inward revealing a narrow stone stairway down into darkness.

I didn't hesitate. I led the way down, keeping the phone's flashlight turned on for Scott's benefit. The werewolves and I didn't need it to see reasonably well in the total darkness underground. At the bottom of the long staircase the stone-lined corridor led away in the direction of the farmhouse. This should take us back to the area beneath the manor's basement.

We kept going until I spotted the glow of a light ahead. I turned off my phone's light and stopped to listen. Rhythmic chanting came from that direction. I moved forward until I reached the end of the passageway. A metal grate closed off the opening, held with an ancient, circular iron padlock. It didn't keep me from seeing what transpired in the large open stone vault on the other side.

Torches lit the room filled with old wooden shelves and wood and metal chests. In the center stood Terrence, resplendent in robes of black and purple. He led the small group of remaining Dark Travelers in a group chant. The room pulsated with power as their voices rose and fell with magical words.

Two of the Travelers held up Gareth from either side. His face was beaten to a bloody pulp and at first, I feared he was dead. One of his eyes cracked open amidst the swelling to glare back at Terrence in defiance. Behind Gareth, another of the Travelers held a long silver rod with a long conical spear tip. He held it pointed at Gareth's back from a few feet away.

At Terrence's feet lay Sadie and Rose. Both were tied up. Rose was bound hand and foot. Sadie appeared to just be secured around her wrists so her hands rested in front of her waist. It didn't matter how they were tied. I couldn't get to them as long as I was locked on this side of the metal grate. I needed to get through.

I gripped the bars and slowly pushed against them so I didn't rattle anything and draw attention to our presence in the corner of the room. Nothing happened. The bars held firm with no give at all.

Warren tapped me on the shoulder. He'd shifted back to human form and now crouched naked beside me. "Hand me your pen knife. I think I can pick that old lock with the smaller blade."

I shifted to the side to make room and dug my knife from my pocket.

Warren took it, opened the smaller, narrow blade and reached through the bars to access the keyhole in the old iron lock. I didn't think we had much chance of unlocking it, but we had to try something.

A soft click thirty seconds later told me I was wrong. Warren handed me back my knife and then slowly removed the lock's hasp from the bolt securing the grate. He pulled it back through the bars and set it quietly on the stone floor.

Scott worked his way forward and whispered in my ear. "The power is building. I can sense it. Something bad is about to happen."

My head whipped around as the chanting grew louder. The two Travelers holding Gareth leaned him forward towards Terrence. At the same time, the one behind the witch hunter drove the silver rod into his back.

Blood fountained from his mouth to splash across Terrence's robes. He didn't seem to care in the slightest. He reached out and gripped the sides of Gareth's head as black energy poured from his mouth, nose, and eyes. The power coursed through the air to envelope Terrence's upper body.

He tensed and howled at the ceiling before lowering his arms to his side. His eyes glowed with a sickly lavender coloring now. The two Travelers holding Gareth let go of him. His body collapsed to the floor, now a withered husk of skin and bone, bereft of life.

"Her next." Terrence pointed at Rose. The two Travelers who'd held Gareth came forward and lifted the struggling form to her feet.

I'd seen enough. There was no way they were killing Rose. It was time to stop this. I turned to my companions, keeping my voice low so it wouldn't be heard over the renewed chanting.

"Warren, you and your friends take the Travelers and free Rose. I'll go for Sadie and get her out of the way. Scott, you have to stop Terrence."

"I don't have that kind of power. He's stronger than I am by far."

"Well, it's too late to worry about that. Come up with something. You're here for a reason. Find it."

I spun around as the chanting increased in tempo and volume again. They had Rose in the same position in which Gareth had been. We were out of time.

I pushed open the grate with a squeal of old metal and ran in leading with my Guardian's sword in front of me. It was go time.

27

Rose

My fuzzy mind cleared quickly when they ran the Ba'al's Lance through Gareth from behind. All my Fae senses burned as if I'd been dipped in magical acid when the dark magic poured from the witch hunter into Terrence.

I tugged at the ropes around my wrists, trying to loosen the knots. It was no use. If anything, my struggles only served to tighten the bonds. I looked over at Sadie and gave her a smile, trying to reassure her. Her half grin didn't do much to hide the terror over what she'd just seen and the effect it had on her. When we got through this, we were going to have to have a long talk about dealing with what she'd witnessed tonight.

I looked back to the basement entrance. I kept hoping to see Chip coming down the stairs with Warren and an army of hairy werewolves. There was little hope of that. They'd never find the magically hidden entrance without knowing where and how to look. If I was going to get out of this, I was going to have to figure it out on my own, as usual.

The two Travelers dropped Gareth's shrunken and shriveled body to the floor. Sadie shrieked, her eyes wide, when he landed a few feet from her.

"Stay strong," I whispered. "Be the Queen you're going to become."

I wasn't sure if she heard me or not and there was no time to talk anymore. Rough hands hoisted me to my feet and dragged me over to stand where Gareth had stood moments before. Without a word to me, Terrence began chanting along with his acolytes.

His eyes glowed with evil, purple energy and I knew he was caught up in the thrall of the power now. I wouldn't be able to talk my way out of this. Of course, there wasn't much I could do. They had me trussed up like a piece of meat. I struggled against my captors as best I could.

The chanting surged louder, and I prepared myself to be skewered by the fell lance.

A shout from the far corner distracted me from my preparations for death. I opened my eyes to see Chip, three werewolves, and Scott the necromancer charging into the room. I didn't know where they'd come from, but I wasn't going to argue the point of their timing. There was one chance now to do something while the warlocks were distracted.

"Use the cant, Sadie. Do it." As I shouted the words, I twisted to the side with all my might and managed to wrench myself free from the Traveler holding my right elbow.

Sadie's eyes brightened as she understood my meaning. She hooked two fingers and beckoned at the overbalanced Traveler reaching out to grab me again.

I continued twisting, turning my head to see the Dark Traveler with the lance thrusting forward at my back. He tried to adjust for my movement at the same instant Sadie pulled the stumbling Traveler completely off balance with her simple spell.

He fell against me, and the lance passed through his side and out through the opposite armpit. Blood poured out of him.

Terrence didn't miss a beat. He jumped forward and grabbed his former acolyte's head, not wanting to waste any of the power escaping from the man's dying body.

Chip arrived in time to lunge forward and thrust his blade at the single Traveler struggling to hold onto my left elbow.

The biker warlock let go and jumped back just in time to avoid being killed by the enchanted blade.

I swung my arms around and held them out as Chip pulled back on the blade. The razor edge sliced neatly between my extended wrists, cutting away the ropes in one slice. I pulled my arms apart, dropping the parted coils of rope to the floor.

"Give me a knife or something to cut my legs free!"

Chip dug in a pocket and came out with a small folding knife. He pressed it into my hands and turned to grab Sadie.

He was too late. Terrence had finished pulling in the power from the hapless Traveler killed by the lance. He leaped in the way and let loose a wave of dark energy at Chip.

Chip brought up his Guardian blade in time to cleave the wave of dark power. It parted and flowed around him like a stream around a boulder.

On the floor, I opened the knife and sawed at the ropes around my knees and ankles, cursing at the time it was taking.

Warren had leaped on the Traveler holding the lance. The biker dropped the silver rod and raised his arms to defend himself against the raging shifter atop him.

Nearby, the three remaining Dark Travelers had their hands full with Warren's two pack mates.

The dark energy of Terrence's spell spent itself and Chip stood up straight, pointing the sword at the dark necromancer. "Let the girl go. Your plan is over."

"Never. I am more powerful now than I've ever been before. Watch and learn, pitiful Guardian."

Terrence pointed at the two shriveled bodies on the floor. The former Gareth and biker both twitched and jerked as the magical commands animated their bodies to stand between Chip and his objective.

Sadie had tried to move away, but Terrence reached down and grabbed her by her hair, yanking her back to his side.

I finally cut through the bonds holding my legs and stood. I looked at the tiny blade and lamented my missing sword, still up in the kitchen above. It would have to do until I could find something else to use.

Chip took a step toward Terrence.

The Fae necromancer jerked at Sadie's hair and held a hand crackling with dark energy over her head. "Don't tempt me, Charles. I would like to keep the Fae Queen alive and let her rule at my side, but I can do without her if you test me."

"Let her go and fight me fair and square," Chip said.

Terrence's head went back as he laughed. "You humans and your pitiful sense of honor. There is no such thing as fair in a fight to the death. The one who cheats, wins. Now, prepare to die and serve me as a corpse like the others."

He swung the empowered hand around to release another spell in our direction.

Chip raised his blade to try and block the power, but I didn't think that would work again. Terrence would try something else this time.

I raised the folding knife back by my ear to try and throw the unbalanced blade in an attempt to distract Terrence.

Before I let go, Scott jumped in front of Chip.

Terrence released the spell a split second later and the dark purple and black energy enveloped the farmer's body instead of Chip.

Scott went rigid for a few seconds then slowly raised his arms up, drawing in the energy around him. Soon he stood with both arms outstretched, pushing back. The two were locked in a magical contest of wills.

Scott shouted over the wail of the coursing energy. "I cannot hold him for long. Get the girl and go while you still can."

Chip shifted and slashed down at the animated corpse of the biker. He lopped off one of the shriveled arms, but the undead creature kept coming.

"Get Sadie, Rose. I'll keep these things busy."

I didn't wait to argue. She was the most important person in this vault right now. I moved to the side. One of the werewolves was down and appeared to be dead since he'd shifted back to his naked human form where he lay on the flagstone floor. The other now fought the remaining two Travelers while Warren still battled with the one who'd wielded the lance.

I darted between Chip, who fought the two animated corpses, and

Warren to race to Sadie's side. I slashed at Terrence's hand gripping her long, dark hair.

Terrence let go, gasping in pain, but unable to stop the test of wills in which he was caught.

I pulled Sadie free and led her to the far corner where Chip had emerged. I spotted the tunnel there. It must be how Chip and the others got down here.

"Go in there, Sadie. It leads back to the farm. Hurry and get away."

"I don't want to go alone, Aunt Rose."

I smiled. "You have to be brave. Your Uncle Chip and I will be up to find you soon. Go and hide and don't come out for anyone but us. Okay?"

Tears streamed down her frightened face, but she nodded and left into the black tunnel back to the surface.

With that taken care of, I could focus on the fighting down here. We needed to end this once and for all.

Chip had his hands full fending off the two reanimated corpses, and I could barely make out Scott in the middle of a swirling cloud of black energy with streaks of purple lightning running through it. The only way I knew the farmer still lived was the presence of the energy circle. If he'd lost, Terrence would have emerged from it to take on the rest of us.

Warren had finished off the biker he fought and had gone to help his pack mate who had been holding off two of the Dark Travelers on her own. Given the situation, I ran to help Chip. He was outnumbered and trying to keep from getting attacked from behind as the animated corpses circled around him.

I didn't have a serious weapon, though. I couldn't wade into a hand-to-hand fight with the withered dead with nothing but a folding pocketknife. My eyes shifted to the floor where the shining silver lance lay beside a dead warlock. I loathed picking up the evil talisman, but realized I didn't have much choice. After all, it wasn't the weapon that was evil, right?

I ran over and bent down to grip the silver shaft. To my surprise, it was warm to the touch despite being kept in a cold cellar like this for centuries. I ignored what the warmth might mean. This was the weapon of a demon from the pits of Hell. If it wanted to run hot, that was fine by me.

By the time I turned around to check on Chip, Gareth's withered corpse had leaped on his back and raked at his shoulders and neck with clawed hands. Chip tried to reach back and pull the attacker away while he fended off the biker corpse attacking from the front.

It was time to get into the action. I darted forward with the precision born of many, many hours of battle both in the training dojo and in actual armed combat. I lined up my strike from the side and lunged with the lance.

The conical point pierced the chest wall of Gareth's corpse. The shrunken head tilted back, and a long, eerie wail came out, followed by a glowing ghostly form that looked just like Gareth did when he was alive. The body that remained released its hold on Chip's back and crumbled away like ash blowing in the wind.

Gareth's ghost pointed at the other corpse, his mouth moving as if he was telling me something. No sound came out, but I got the gist of what he wanted me to do.

I stepped around to Chip's side and lunged again, striking the shriveled biker corpse in the chest with the lance. Once again, the creature wailed in agony and a ghostly form emerged. The body, freed of its animation energy, crumbled away just like the other one.

The ghost of the biker floated a few inches off the floor for a second then turned and flew away to pass through the ceiling. Apparently, it didn't want to stick around for the end of the fight.

Warren and the other werewolf had finished off the final two bikers while Chip and I had fought the corpses. They came over to stand beside us. We all stared at the battle that raged in the center of the vault. The swirling ball of necromantic energy filled the air with static electricity so that wisps of our hair floated up from our heads. It must have been really irritating to the fur-covered werewolves.

"What do we do now?" Chip asked. "I can't tell if Scott is winning or losing."

I knew what he meant. I could barely pick out which form was which in the center of the swirling mass.

I shrugged. "I don't know. Gareth told us we needed a necromancer to beat Terrence. Maybe we just have to let this battle play out."

Gareth's ghost floated over until it passed in front of me. It pointed at me and then at the swirling globe of energy.

I cocked my head to one side, puzzled at what he was trying to say. "I can't go into that, Gareth. Even with my Fae resistance, that much energy would fry me."

Gareth shook his head and pointed at me again, then pantomimed shoving something into the whirling ball. He repeated his series of gestures again and again, getting more frantic by the second. Whatever he wanted me to do, he wanted me to do it right away.

Chip snapped his fingers. "The lance! He wants you to stab it in there. Maybe it will draw off the energy?"

Gareth shook his head and pointed again at the swirling energy. He held a flattened hand a few inches over his head and pointed at the cloud again.

It hit me and I cursed aloud. It had taken me too long to figure it out. "Shit, you want me to stab Terrence with the lance through the energy ball?"

Gareth smiled and nodded.

"Will that work?" Chip asked.

"Look what it did to the animated corpses out here," I said. "Maybe it will siphon his power away from him and allow Scott to win the battle."

"You must hurry," Warren snarled. He pointed at the shadowy forms of the two combatants inside the ball of power.

I saw what he meant right away. The shorter of the two shadow forms inside the cloud, who must be Scott, had stumbled and seemed stooped now as if weakened. He was losing the fight.

Without hesitation, I charged forward, leveling the lance at my hip. Trusting my instincts, I thrust through the swirling clouds of energy at where I thought I could see the taller of the two figures inside. I hoped I was right.

The conical point of the lance pierced the cloud, creating a tunnel through the energy as it went. I pressed in, stretching out my arms as far as they would go.

Finally, I felt resistance and I lunged with all the force I could muster. The lance's tip slid into something, and the shaft jerked in my hands as whomever I'd struck on the other end struggled.

Another wail, similar to the others we'd heard, but far louder, echoed around the cavernous vault. I held onto the jerking silver shaft with all my strength while the wailing continued.

The swirling energy cloud dissipated in an instant as if a strong breeze had come and wafted it away. It revealed Terrence and Scott standing facing each other. Scott looked as if he'd aged forty years. He easily looked like he was a hundred years old.

Terrence looked much, much worse. He had the look of the shriveled corpses and had shrunken down to barely four and half feet tall. He stood transfixed on the end of the Ba'al's Lance, his mouth working as if trying to say something. Then his body went limp, and he fell to the floor, sliding off the end of the lance as he did.

Scott staggered to the side and would have fallen to the flagstone floor if Chip hadn't rushed forward to catch him. His breathing came in wheezing gasps, and he let loose with a series of rattling coughs that shook his whole, frail body.

Chip lowered the aged necromancer to the floor and gently pulled his hands free from beneath his shoulders.

I handed the lance to Warren to hold, and I came over to kneel beside the old farmer. "Scott, hold on. We can get you to the hospital. We'll find you some help."

He reached up and gripped my hand in his. His paper-thin skin made it feel like I was gripping the hand of a skeleton.

"It is best this way. I realize now that a life of undeath is not something my Darcy would want. Now I can rest beside her in a far better place."

He struggled to breathe and coughed several times trying to clear his rattling lungs. I waited for him to regather his strength.

"Rose, promise me you'll have me laid to rest beside my Darcy in a peaceful place at our farm. You'll find her body in the chest freezer in the basement of the farmhouse."

I hid disgust rising within me at what he'd done. It was best to remember him for what he did here to help us save Sadie. In the end, he'd done the right thing and come to the right conclusion about his dark magical ventures.

"What about the zombies at the farm?" Chip asked. "We can't let them get free to wreak havoc on the community."

"They will be free to act on their own once I'm dead. Find them homes with others of their kind. They can live out their existence in peace without me exerting my will over them." He looked back at me. "Don't forget your promise to me, Rose."

"I won't. Be at peace, Scott. You and Darcy will be together again soon."

Scott smiled and let out one last ragged breath. He was gone a second later.

"Let's go and get Sadie," I said as I stood. I wiped away a tear running down my cheek and hoped Chip didn't see it.

"Where is she?" Chip asked as he looked around the vault. "I know she's close, but my connection with her is still fuzzy, even with Terrence gone."

"I sent her back up the tunnel you used to come down here."

Chip wiped off his blade with a strip of T-shirt from one of the dead bikers. "Then let's get out of here and go get her. She needs to sleep in her own bed tonight."

"Agreed," I said. I lifted the lance and pointed across the room to a stone alcove. "Warren, put this back on the rack over there. Then call in some help to come and clean up this mess. Make sure they're reliable. My aunt will inventory the contents of the vault. She'll hold you accountable for anything that turns up missing."

"There is no need for that, princess," Reston said from the stairs up to the manor's basement. "I will take care of the restitution of this place. There is no need to involve more outsiders."

The flush of embarrassment at getting caught like this washed over my face. "Reston, how did you know about this?" I looked at Chip, knowing he must be responsible.

The butler shook his head. "There is a magical alarm on the vault's entrance. I knew someone had accessed it long before the Guardian called me. Now if you will replace the lance and leave to find young Sadie, I will begin my work."

Warren nodded and took the lance to put it away. Chip and I waited until he'd finished, then we all left Reston to handle the cleanup. We walked quickly, both Chip and I trying to be the first to get to our niece and make sure she was okay. After all, she was the most important thing of tonight's rescue.

28

Chip

"Sadie, honey, you're going to be late for school." I called for her up the stairs while I held her jacket and backpack.

"Coming, Uncle Chip."

I waited patiently, savoring having her back home again. Luckily, we'd had the rest of the weekend to recover a little and make sure she was truly all right. Bernard had a couple of rough nights dealing with a few particularly bad nightmares. He told me about them, and I decided I'd talk to Rose about seeking some sort of Unusual counselor Sadie could talk to for a few sessions. It couldn't hurt for her to get some help dealing with a kidnapping by a murderous relative.

"What's the look for, Uncle Chip?" Sadie asked. She'd bounced down the stairs while I was lost in my worried thoughts.

"Just thinking about the last few days, Sadie. You know, I can make it so you take a few more days off from school if you want."

"No, I want to go back with my friends. Astrid called me twice over the weekend. She's not avoiding me anymore."

"You didn't tell her what happened, did you?"

She shook her head, her braid swinging back and forth behind her head. "No, I stuck to the story of me having a really bad case of the flu."

"Good. It wouldn't do for anyone to know what happened. Even telling a really good friend could lead to trouble for us."

She smiled and slipped on her jacket, then grabbed her backpack from me. "I know, Uncle Chip. I do hope that someday I can tell someone about our family. It's hard keeping the secret."

"I know, sweetie. It's hard on me, too. I can only imagine what it must be like for you. It's for the best, I promise."

"What's for the best?" Rose asked. She'd come in via the front door.

"Keeping the family secret, Rose. Sadie was saying how hard it is for her."

Rose came over and kneeled in front of her niece. "I know exactly what you mean. Your mommy and I had to keep the secret all through school, too. It's not easy, but if you tell the wrong person, you end up putting all of us in danger. What happened before the weekend was an example of that. Once someone knows your destiny, they can't help but want to take some of that power and influence for themselves."

"I know, Aunt Rose. I was just saying it's hard to not tell my friends. I need someone to share this with besides you all."

Addy interrupted us as he scrambled around the corner and saluted. "I can keep the secret, too."

I reached out and tousled his hair. "I know you can, buddy. Now let's go and get you two back on the bus so Sadie can get to school and see all her friends again."

Rose joined us as we all walked out the front door and headed to the end of the street where the bus stop was. The kids scampered down the walk and joined their friends walking towards the corner. Ellie and Barbara waved at Rose and me.

"There's a soccer game this Saturday morning, right?" Rose asked.

"Yes," I replied. "And practice tonight, Wednesday, and Thursday. Care to take a shift and take Sadie to it so Addy and I can have a guys' night this Thursday?"

"I can do that," Rose said. "Sadie and I can make it a girls' night and go get a treat after practice."

Sadie turned back at the mention of a treat. "Ooo, I can't wait, Aunt Rose. Can we invite Astrid to come along?"

I caught the hint of a grimace that Rose covered well at the mention of her high school nemesis' child. "Sure, honey. If that's what you want, then Astrid can join us. I'll call her mom and set it up."

I smiled at that. The things we parental types did for our kids. I took a deep breath and savored the crisp fall air. I didn't mind the work. It turned out being Uncle Chip was my destiny and I was okay with all of it.

Be ready for more coming in March 2025 with *Summer Break Fae, book 4 in Uncle Chip Saves the Fae.*

Also by Jamie Davis

Get a free book and updates for new books.
visit JamieDavisBooks.com/send-free-book/

Extreme Medical Services Series

(A 9-book Urban Fantasy series starting with)

Book 1 - Extreme Medical Services

—

Eldara Sister Series

The Nightingale's Angel

Blue and Gray Angel

—

Lone Wolf Squadron Series

(a 9-book Space Western series starting with)

Marshal the Stars

—

The Huntress Clan Saga

(A 6-book Urban Fantasy series starting with)

Huntress Initiate

—

The Broken Throne Series

(A 5-Book Dystopian Urban Fantasy

starting with)

The Charm Runner

—

The Accidental Traveler LitRPG Series

(with C.J. Davis)

(A 6-book Epic Fantasy Series starting with)

The Accidental Thief

—

Follow on Facebook for updates, news, and upcoming book excerpts

Jamie's Fun Fantasy Readers Facebook Group

Help the Author

I Need Your Help ...

Without reviews indie books like this one are almost impossible to market.

Leaving a review will only take a minute — it doesn't have to be long or involved, just a sentence or two that tells people what you liked about the book, to help other readers know why they might like it, too. It also helps me write more of what you love.

The truth is, VERY few readers leave reviews. Please help me out by being the exception.

Thank you in advance!

Jamie Davis

About the Author

Jamie Davis, RN, NRP, B.A., A.S., is a nationally recognized medical educator who began educating new emergency responders as a training officer for his local EMS program. As a media producer, he has been recognized for the <u>MedicCast Podcast</u> (<u>MedicCast.com/blog</u>), a weekly program for emergency medical providers like EMTs and paramedics, and the Nursing Show, a similar program for nurses and nursing students. His programs and resources have been downloaded over 6 million times by listeners and viewers.

Jamie lives and writes at his home in Maryland. He lives in the woods with his wife, three children, and a dog.

Follow Jamie Online
www.jamiedavisbooks.com